Riverwood Hollow

A PLACE FOR DREAMING

Meredith Eastwood

authorHOUSE®

AuthorHouse™
1663 Liberty Drive
Bloomington, IN 47403
www.authorhouse.com
Phone: 833-262-8899

Published by AuthorHouse 08/25/2021

ISBN: 978-1-6655-3642-4 (sc)
ISBN: 978-1-6655-3641-7 (e)

Library of Congress Control Number: 2021917503

Print information available on the last page.

This book is printed on acid-free paper.

In memory of Thomas Jay Eastwood

Children treasure the hope that they might be like the children in books: secretly magical, part of some deeper, mysterious world that makes them something out of the ordinary.

—Helen Macdonald, *H is for Hawk*

Contents

Chapter 1

The Airport Gift Shop

Believe there is a great power silently
working all things for good,
behave yourself and never mind the rest.

—Beatrix Potter, *Merry Christmas, Peter Rabbit*

The gift shop in the Seattle-Tacoma International Airport sparkled with seasonal displays to attract last-minute Christmas shoppers. Tiny, white lights draped around the windows illuminated displays of angels, candles, Santa statues, stuffed polar bears, and assorted knickknacks. Scents of pine, cinnamon, and peppermint filled the air, and passengers wandered through the aisles seeking special gifts. In the middle of the toy section stood a puppet tree. Several animal puppets hung from wooden pegs, but they weren't ordinary puppets. Each of them had a name except the squirrel. When no one was looking, they engaged in conversations with one another.

*

The squirrel puppet exhaled a deep sigh, dreaming of an escape from the peg on which he hung. "Deck the Halls" was playing again.

He had memorized all the Christmas songs that repeated on the gift shop's sound system. It wasn't too difficult to remember the words, since it was his second Christmas being suspended on the same wooden tree. He couldn't remember how he had arrived at the airport store, and one day melted into the next. The holidays lifted his spirits, but it was his dreams of another world that brought him the promise of excitement and adventure. In his dreams, he escaped the fake puppet tree in the gift shop and became a real squirrel in a forest of real trees.

When he was awake in his ordinary life, the squirrel accepted his place among the other animal puppets displayed on the gift shop tree. Each of them had their designated spots. Wings, a hawk, was perched at the top of the tree. The squirrel hung below Wings next to a monarch butterfly, where he hoped to attract the attention of shoppers. Roar, a lion, and Bandita, a raccoon, rested on the pegs in the middle of the tree. An opossum known as Pinkie, a painted turtle named Shelltin, and many other creatures dangled near the bottom of tree where it was easy for small children to pull them from their pegs. Fire, a dragon, sat on the bottom peg at the tree's base.

Because Fire claimed the ability to fly, the squirrel wondered why the dragon had been placed at the bottom of the tree. Fire told him he was the wisest of them all, and therefore, he anchored the tree as the guardian for their community of puppets. Though Roar sat on a peg in the middle of the tree, he claimed the role of leadership. He kept watch over things happening in the gift shop. He also did a fair amount of bragging, calling himself the king of the puppet animals.

The squirrel liked to observe the passengers waiting for flights as they wandered through the shop. The children played with the toys and games. Both kids and adults created performances with the popular puppets, ones that had names. Most of the time, the squirrel felt ignored, left hanging by his bushy red tail as children and their parents inserted their hands into the mouths and limbs of Fire, Roar, and Wings. He wondered why he had been left out of the fun.

Each time he managed a glimpse of the tag attached to his tail, he hoped he would see a name assigned to him. When none of the store managers noticed the oversight, the other animals agreed that his name should be Squirrel. He wanted a name like Tree Climber! Secretly, he wondered if he wasn't important enough to have a name.

Sometimes a clerk moved Squirrel to a display shelf next to the children's books. He enjoyed those days, looking at the colorful covers of books about animals and kids having fun in mysterious places outside the airport. There were two books about rabbits, *The Complete Adventures of Peter Rabbit* and *The Velveteen Rabbit*.

There was a book about a monkey called *Curious George* and a book popular at Christmastime, *How the Grinch Stole Christmas.*

Squirrel was most curious about a book called *The Jungle Book.* He once heard a mother tell her child about a brown bear named Bagheera, a fierce tiger named Shere Khan, and a boy named Mowgli. Squirrel wanted to meet a little boy like the jungle child who would be his friend.

Every night when the store was quiet, Squirrel slept. He dreamed about racing down a rock-strewn path through an emerald forest sprinkled with yellow wildflowers. He dreamed about chasing blue butterflies, digging for buried treasure, and leaping from one tree branch to another. Sometimes he dreamed about sitting next to a child who read stories to him about heroes and talking animals.

After he emerged from sleep, Squirrel felt puzzled, not quite understanding where he had gone during his dreams or exactly what a dream really was. Stranger still, he had no idea how he was able to give names to the things he saw and the events he experienced during his excursions in the forest.

With Christmas Eve just a few days away, Squirrel had become more concerned about his waking life. Hundreds of travelers were shopping the area around the puppet tree. The rabbit, mouse, and bear had already been purchased. When he watched the clerk gift wrap special toys and books with shiny silver paper and tie red ribbons around the necks of the puppets, he knew they were presents for lucky children.

Last year during the holidays, nearly all the puppets went to new homes, but Squirrel had been left sitting on a peg next to Shelltin when the new shipments arrived early in January. Squirrel felt sad that he and the turtle had not been chosen last Christmas. This year, he hoped the clerk would tie red ribbons around their necks.

Chapter 2

Waiting to be Chosen

Maybe Christmas, he thought,
doesn't come from a store.
Maybe Christmas...perhaps...means a little more!

—Dr. Seuss, *How the Grinch Stole Christmas!*

One morning while "Jingle Bells" played in the gift shop, Squirrel was awakened from his sleep adventures by a gravelly voice.

"Hey, Squirrel, are you dreaming again?"

"Wh ... what? Who said that?" Squirrel called out to the other puppets as he felt a paw yanking his tail.

"It's me, Roar," growled the lion.

"Ouch! I should have guessed it was you, Roar," Squirrel said. "Always taking charge of things, even my tail. I was playing in the forest, and it was the best dream ever."

Roar laughed. "Who cares about dreams? What the lion says in this gift shop is more important than fanciful visions, and everyone is supposed to listen. Especially when you're the king of the puppet tree."

Squirrel nodded, remembering how often he ignored the lion, but he decided to reply with words Roar wanted to hear. "Roar, we always pay attention to what you say."

"My goodness, the little squirrel wants to climb trees," Bandita chittered, her eyes glaring at Squirrel through her black mask. "I remember when a kid told me how raccoons are so smart they can open doors. I learned from that boy how resourceful I could be, able to get into and out of places closed to most animals. That sounds like something I'd like to be doing—breaking out of this gift shop. Maybe exploring that woodsy dream world of yours, Squirrel. I can almost visualize the trees over my head."

Pinkie dropped her thin, furless tail over the peg where she sat and leaned her head toward the conversation. "There's a good reason why we're here in this gift shop. We're spirit animals. We comfort and protect the children who adopt us. Each of us is the right animal puppet for a special child."

"So, I'm king of spirit animals too!" Roar boasted, fluffing his mane with his right paw.

"Could everyone stop talking so fast?" snapped a voice Squirrel knew belonged to the turtle.

"Shhhh … smoke on the horizon," whispered Fire. "I see kids."

As two girls approached the puppet tree with cries of delight, Squirrel twitched his whiskers, feeling a surge of excitement. Yet the girls didn't seem to notice. The taller of the girls with long, blonde hair wore a lacy pink dress and hooded black raincoat. She grabbed the dragon. Squirrel watched her slide a hand into Fire's wide belly. Suddenly, the dragon's mouth opened and closed. Squirrel guessed her fingers had reached into Fire's jaw.

The girl raised Fire above her head and raced through the store. Squirrel watched the dragon's mouth gape open with the words of the girl's imagination as his wide, iridescent blue wings fluttered past the candy counter. When the girl rounded the puppet tree again, Fire's eyes bulged green while he exhaled the breath of the girl's promise, "My wings carry me above the winter clouds through the starry sky."

"Dear Dragon," the girl shouted, "we'll fly away into magical Snoqualmie forest, where there's an ice castle on a mountaintop, and I'll be your Princess Catherine."

Fire's mouth moved with the girl's dragon-like voice and guiding hand. "On my back you shall ride, Your Majesty."

When Squirrel could no longer see Fire's face, he pictured the gleam in the dragon's eyes, knowing what he was really saying in his mind to the girl. Something like, *Hey, put me down. I'm not too interested in an ice castle. I would melt it all with the fire in my belly. And I'd rather be ridden by a courageous heroine than by a girl pretending to be a princess.*

Squirrel admired the way Fire expressed himself with an edgy sense of humor. He wished he had a special talent. He didn't have wings or a powerful voice, and he couldn't even pretend to spit flames at passing tourists.

Interrupting Squirrel's thoughts, a hand plucked him from his peg, and his body began to move. The smaller girl, also blonde and dressed in pink with a shiny black coat, had inserted her thumb and fingers into his paws and mouth. They began to move. The girl skipped around the toy shelves, and Squirrel began yanking small stuffed animals from their places. His mouth moved up and down with words only a small child would think of saying.

"Hello, little bunny. It's me, your best friend," the little girl squealed in a pretend squirrel voice. "Oh, teddy bear, how would you like to play in the woods with me?" Then, looking into Squirrel's face, she said in her little-girl voice, "Little squirrel, you'll come home with me, and I'll love you forever."

Squirrel felt a warm glow spread through his body, thinking his lucky day had finally arrived. When the little girl danced around the puppet tree, Squirrel winked at Roar. He knew the lion had been watching the events of the morning unfold.

"How sweet, the word *love*," Roar grumbled. "In the real world, love can be quite disappointing. Personally, I'm rather fond of the word *courage*."

Squirrel ignored Roar's remarks. He wondered if the little girl had heard them. But it didn't matter because he knew he was about to be purchased. This girl would carry him on one of the big airplanes he'd seen through the wide window across the corridor from the gift shop. He was going to fly. What a grand adventure it would be.

In the very next moment, his hopes were dashed when a woman, also blonde and dressed in a black raincoat, rushed toward the girl. "Catherine, put that squirrel down. Your sister has chosen the dragon. We can only afford one puppet today. You two will have to share."

Squirrel hit the floor headfirst when Catherine dropped him. As the girls disappeared behind their mother, he lay on the gray carpet beneath the puppet tree, peering up at the knowing smile on Roar's face. Feeling rejected, Squirrel closed his eyes and whispered, "She said she'd love me forever."

"You must have courage," Roar said. "It's the truest quality of the heart. You may believe you're only a squirrel, not as important as Fire. It may seem like humans prefer the bigger animals, ones that roar, fly, or spit fire. But there'll come a time when someone will appreciate your trickster gifts."

As Squirrel was pondering Roar's words about courage and his trickster gifts, a clerk picked him up and hung him on a peg next to the hawk at the top of the tree.

"It's a good thing you didn't have to spend the day on the floor," Wings said with what Squirrel understood was a measure of kindness. "I remember that word, *love*. Sadly, many in the world are too busy for things like love. When I fly across the sky in my dreams, I watch humans go from one thing to the next, not paying much attention to the people or things around them. Most of them don't see what's really important. I bet they've lost their dreams."

"Wings, do you have dreams too?" Squirrel asked, meeting the hawk's unwavering gaze.

"I don't like to share my dreams because other animals laugh. But all of us dream. Some don't remember, and many don't want to admit it because they're afraid of what the dreams might mean. Some just don't take the time to pay attention to them."

Squirrel was relieved hearing Wing's words. "I never knew

everyone dreamed, but Fire once told me he had dreams. He said that the messages in dreams were important. And now he's gone."

"Maybe there's a message in this experience," Wings said. "Can you imagine living with those girls? I bet Fire will be smoked out within the month and tossed with their old dolls and stuffed animals into a basement storage box. I'm guessing that the girls will play with the latest movie characters, and Fire will be forgotten."

"I will not give up on my dreams. I know there's a world outside this store. I've seen it in my dreams, and someday I'll find it."

"It's a good day for watching and waiting. Think about where we might end up if each of us left this store with a child."

"Yeah, we'd be taken away from our friends, perhaps never seeing one another again," Bandita said. "And I'm rather fond of you and your dreaming adventures."

The hawk folded his wings toward his fluffy white chest feathers. "In my view, being perched on our tree is better than being left alone in the bottom of a toy box. Plus, I suspect that many kids think those Lego sets are more interesting to play with than a stuffed puppet."

Pinkie grinned, flashing a row of sharp white teeth. "Hey, Squirrel, you can always dream of a woodsy place and hang out there without plastic toys."

Squirrel wished he could drop a nut on Pinkie's head. "I don't believe every child would discard a puppet animal to be replaced by movie characters."

"You dream too much, Squirrel," Roar said, shaking his mane. "In the meantime, try to imagine our puppet tree as a tree of life."

"Please slow down," Shelltin snapped. "I can hardly keep up with this conversation."

Squirrel flicked his tail, irritated by the advice from his friends. "Some tree of life! All I ever do is hang on a peg, watching customers shop and look at their smartphones."

"Yeah, I've noticed those little phones," Bandita said, drawing her paw across her chest. "Little do they understand the ways of the heart."

Shelltin stuck his head out from his shell again. "Roar talks about his courageous heart. But, Bandita, you've got a huge heart imprinted on your chest."

Squirrel looked at the hawk. "Fire has been purchased. Wings, you must be our new guardian and keep watch for all of us now."

"Hey, that's my job!" roared the lion. "I watch everything."

Wings lifted his long, striped tail feathers. "But, Roar, do you see everything?"

That night, Squirrel thought about his dreams. He was determined to figure out more about the dream world. Maybe he would discover his name there too. And that word *love*; he knew it was an important word. Someday he would understand what it meant. For now, he had his friends, all hanging on their little tree of life, except for Fire.

Chapter 3

Lucky Day

Open your heart. Someone will come.
Someone will come for you.
But first you must open your heart.

—Kate DiCamillo, *The Miraculous
Journey of Edward Tulane*

Dazzling sunlight splashed through the leafy trees of a summer forest. Squirrel enjoyed days like this in his dream world. He scurried around the ground, sampling an assortment of nuts, acorns, and seeds. Then he ran to a towering tree whose broad branches arched over a sandy path. Digging his sharp claws into the gnarled trunk, he climbed toward the top. Satisfied with the view, he crept to the end of a large limb and paused to survey the woodland he had entered.

Squirrel couldn't believe what he saw next. Below him, Roar wandered along the shore of a muddy river that flowed under a covered bridge downstream. He looked much too small to be a lion, and his mane had shrunk to little more than an orange ring around his neck. Bandita sat in the middle of a group of tall orange flowers on the banks of the river. She turned her head this way and that, looking as though she was confused. Pinkie huddled beneath an iron bench. The old bench leaned against a flowering tree whose lower branches dipped beneath the river's flowing water. Shelltin floated on the water's surface next to a partially submerged log.

Curious about the appearance of his friends, Squirrel turned toward a small cottage that faced the river, looking for Wings. The hawk was perched on a birdbath, watching a blue jay flutter around a bird feeder. Squirrel had seen feeders before in his dreams. They were good places to find seeds and corn cobs. He also had learned about blue jays. They always chased him away from the food.

Squirrel dashed back along the branch to the trunk and descended the tree, swishing his tail for balance. Just a few feet from the ground, he leaped. He felt his tail inflate before landing on all four paws. Delighted with this newfound skill, he called out to the lion.

*

Squirrel heard Roar's words as he opened his eyes on the puppet tree in the gift shop. "Hey, Squirrel, wake up! You're barking in your sleep."

"Huh ... oh yeah, I was dreaming," he murmured, blinking his eyes when the lion's face appeared.

"It's time to look sharp! Travelers are arriving for the morning flights," Roar said. "It's Christmastime. You want to find a home, don't you?"

"Yeah, but I was having the best dream. I ran through the grass in the woods and ate crunchy nuts and seeds. Then I climbed up high in a huge tree. I saw a bridge over a muddy river, a path through tall orange flowers, and a little cottage with bird feeders. And everything smelled sweet and tasty. You were there, Roar ... and Wings, Bandita, Pinkie, even Shelltin. I was so happy. Maybe that's what love's about, being with friends in a place where you feel at home."

"Slow down, Squirrel," Shelltin pleaded. "Now where was I in that dream world of yours?"

"You were floating in the river, near a mossy log that had fallen from one of the trees. You were hardly moving."

Roar howled with laughter. "Of course he was hardly moving. What would you expect from a turtle? More importantly, what would a lion like me be doing in the woods? I'm not some small house cat hunting mice in the forest. Squirrel, you must get grounded. Dreams are only dreams. They're not the real world. Reality is here in this store!"

"I know, I know," Squirrel said. "You keep telling me that. But my dreams feel so real, and I'm a real squirrel in them." He decided to keep silent about how Roar appeared in his dream.

Roar continued to laugh. "Well, you can't live your life like a dream."

"I've said this before. I'd rather live in a dream than spend my life hanging on a hook in a store."

Just as Squirrel spit out the last word, a sticky hand grabbed him. Bright blue eyes on a boy's gleeful face stared down at him as he felt fingers slide into his puppet mouth. The boy giggled as he made Squirrel's mouth move up and down and his paws back and forth.

"Squirrel," the boy said, "you and I could have so much fun climbing trees. I love to climb trees."

When Squirrel took a closer look at the boy, he noticed his sandy brown hair was swept to the side as though he'd just combed it. The boy's red jacket was unzipped, revealing a blue T-shirt with a Superman symbol on the front. A black backpack covered in superhero stickers hung over his left shoulder. Judging by his many days observing children playing with the puppets, Squirrel thought the boy was about ten years old.

Squirrel had seen superhero toys and stickers during his time in the gift shop. He even knew some of the characters' stories, having heard conversations among the children who clutched the toy figures in their hands. *Thank goodness I don't see the boy holding a smartphone.*

Please choose me, Squirrel hoped. Silent conversations only seemed to work among the puppets. But perhaps a special child could hear his wish.

The boy tapped the arm of a woman wearing a heavy wool coat. "Mom, can I have this puppet? It reminds me of the story you read to me about Squirrel Nutkin when I was a little boy."

The boy's mother pushed a strand of dark, curly hair behind her ear and peered down at him. "Why, yes, Travis. This puppet does look like Nutkin. I know you remember that the tale about Nutkin was written by Beatrix Potter. I think the squirrel puppet would be a fun travel companion for you on our flights to Grandma Floi's house. I already have a copy of Potter's *The Complete Tales* in my suitcase. It's one of the gifts I plan to give your cousins."

Squirrel relaxed into the boy's hug as he continued listening to the conversation between the boy and his mother.

"Mom, look at this book about Norse mythology."

"I saw it. Ratatoskr is another tricky squirrel, and he's in that book. I think we should get this book too."

21

"I remember that story. Ratatoskr ran up and down Yggdrasil, the World Tree, passing messages between the eagle at the top and the dragon in the roots."

"Actually, Ratatoskr was more of a troublemaker, spreading gossip and discord between the eagle and the dragon."

"I liked that squirrel. He was very mischievous," the boy said. "I remember one time when you and dad took me hiking in the woods. We saw a squirrel running up and down an old oak tree, barking at us. I thought he was Ratatoskr."

The boy's mother smiled. "I remember that time at Grandma's house. She always talks about that swamp chestnut oak being as old as the state itself, a sapling in 1816. And there's another massive tree at the end of that trail near her cottage, a sycamore that spreads its branches over the entire river. I'm certain that it is even older. I still imagine that towering, ancient tree looking like a world tree, what people also call a tree of life."

Squirrel felt his ears perk up. *There's a real tree of life?*

"Wow! There's *The Jungle Book*!" The boy exclaimed. "It was a really good movie."

"Travis, I know how much you love your books. I have an idea. I'll get that book too. That way, each of you kids will receive a special book on Christmas morning. I think I have room in my carry-on bag, though it'll be pretty heavy."

Squirrel had heard the boy's name a couple times. *Travis sounds like a nice name.*

As the mother was talking to Travis, Squirrel glanced back at Roar hanging on the puppet tree. The lion frowned, and Squirrel's throat tightened. He regretted leaving behind the only friends he had known.

While his mother stood in line at the checkout counter, Travis ran back to the puppet tree with Squirrel still tucked under his arm. Squirrel wondered if Travis was going to return him in exchange for another animal. Instead, Squirrel felt the boy's hands slip inside his head and then into one of his paws. Facing his puppet companions still dangling on their pegs, he was able to wave goodbye.

"Goodbye, lion, hawk, turtle, raccoon, opossum, and all you other animals," Travis said, moving the squirrel's mouth. Then Travis added his own farewell. "I wish I could take all of you with me. I promise, the squirrel is going to a good home ... a forever home."

Shelltin stuck his head out from beneath his shell ever so slightly. "I'll always remember you, little squirrel," he whispered.

Squirrel heard the thump of the boy's heart as he leaned his head against the Superman T-shirt. *Courage,* he thought. *It takes courage to travel to a new home.*

Although the clerk had not tied a red ribbon around his neck, Squirrel knew he had finally been chosen because he was a special puppet. When Travis walked toward the store's exit, Squirrel glimpsed Fire in a box on the floor next to the cash register. He was sitting on top of a collection of items, including leather gloves, a red candle, and a Santa statue.

Then Squirrel heard Roar's last words. "Maybe sometimes dreams come true."

Chapter 4

This World or the Dream?

Today is your day. Your mountain is
waiting. So get on your way.

—Dr. Seuss, *Oh, the Places You'll Go!*

Lightning flashed, illuminating the blustery sway of the trees overlooking the river. A few seconds later, the ground shook with rumbling thunder, and water began to fall from the sky. Squirrel shivered and shook his tail, trying to toss off the moisture collecting on his fur. From his branch at the top of an old oak tree, he clutched an acorn in his paws and watched the rapidly moving line of storm clouds. The branch on which he sat thrashed wildly, almost tossing him to the ground. He dropped the nut, dug his claws into the rough bark, and looked down at his friends.

Roar crouched within purple-flowered ground cover. He still looked too small to be a lion. Squirrel could only imagine the thoughts of disgust that were coursing through Roar's mind. He was stuck outside in pouring rain rather than watching over the animals on a tree of life in his gift store kingdom.

Bandita's masked face couldn't hide her alarm. She had ducked into a crevice beneath the trunk of a fallen tree. Her liquid eyes peered over a row of tiny mushrooms. "Hey, Squirrel, it's time to hide. This is no place for a puppet. If this windy, wet forest is your dream world, I'd rather be hanging on a dry puppet tree."

"If this is what it's like being real, I agree with the raccoon," Roar added, shaking water from his dirty face. "I detest getting wet."

"But you're my friends," Squirrel called through the noise of the falling rain. "This place is usually sunny and warm."

Bandita blinked her eyes and yelled, "Silly Squirrel, this dream is more like a nightmare." She crawled out from beneath her hiding spot and threw up her paws. "It's time for me to leave you." Squirrel knew that on a moonlit night, she would have wanted to climb his tree.

"Bye, bye, Squirrel. Stay safe," growled Roar. "I'm going back to the puppet tree."

"Please don't leave me," Squirrel barked over the howl of the wind.

*

Squirrel rubbed his eyes and peeked out from the back pocket of the boy's backpack. A crowd of noisy passengers were standing in the waiting area near one of the departure gates. *I've been dreaming*, he thought. *My friends were in my dreams again. And I've had dreams about storms before where I was sitting in a tree with a nut in my paws. That place must be real, just like Fire once told me.* Squirrel sighed, recalling a conversation he had with Fire weeks ago when the gift shop had been closed. The other puppets had been sound asleep when the dragon awakened him from a dream like the one he just experienced. Squirrel closed his eyes, recalling the memory.

"Squirrel, wake up. You're dreaming!" Fire had exclaimed.

"Huh, what?" Squirrel mumbled, flicking his tail.

"You've been making those annoying clucking noises again and swishing your big tail."

"Oh, Fi … Fire, it feels so real, the place where I go when I'm sleeping."

"It's another world where you live in your dreams, and it is a real place," Fire said. "I know because I've been there myself. It's the dream world."

"The dream world? Where is it? I'm always in a forest. Sometimes the trees have leaves. This time, I was on a tree branch without leaves. I had something good to eat, a huge acorn. It smelled delicious. But all of a sudden, the sky lit up with bright streaks of light, and a thundering noise shook the ground. Then the wind blew, and water dropped through the branches. I had to grasp the bark to keep from falling into a pile of leaves on the ground."

Fire puffed out a thin trail of smoke from his mouth. "It's difficult to explain what happens in the dream world. The water is called rain. It's one version of what humans define as weather. It happens outside the airport." Fire paused. The next stream of smoke from his mouth wafted over the entire puppet tree.

"How do you do that?" asked Squirrel. "How come no one sees it?"

"What? You mean the smoke? It's magic. You must have imagination to see the magic that's invisible to most animals and humans. You most definitely have imagination, Squirrel, if you can see my smoke."

"But where's the dream world?"

"Oh yes, we got off the subject with my puffing," replied the dragon. "The way I've experienced it, the dream world is the place that breathes fire into your soul. It's an imaginal realm where each animal and human discovers their true home. For you, it's a forest where animals like you climb trees, play, and chitter at every passerby. Where they scamper about collecting and storing supplies for later use. Our dreams contain important messages that we need to pay attention to, and the dream world is a real place. You can return there anytime you want."

"Fire, do you really dream too?"

The dragon's eyes glistened red as he continued. "Yes, of course I dream. Sometimes I don't remember everything that happens in them. Most of the time, I dream about friends in my life that I care about. Sometimes they actually join me in the dream world."

"But what about this world, the one in the gift shop with my friends on the puppet tree? Isn't this place the real world?"

Fire exhaled a long trail of rainbow-colored smoke, meeting Squirrel's eyes. "There are many worlds. Try to think of our gift shop where we are living as one of the worlds inside the airport. There's a café next door and a clothing store down the corridor. Each of those places is a separate world, different from ours. There are other worlds outside the airport and even outside the city of Seattle. I wish I could fly on one of the silver birds to those worlds beyond the Seattle world. If you ask me, your dream world is as real as you want it to be. And perhaps this world around the puppet tree is less real than we think it is."

"Fire, you always have a complicated way of saying things,"

Squirrel said, feeling a rumble in his stomach. "It's a scary thought, flying away to somewhere you've never seen before."

Fire puffed several smoke rings that drifted toward the ceiling like a spiral. "Yes, but there's a deep desire in every animal to live and grow in his or her right place. Sometimes your imagination takes you there. That's one of the reasons you dream. You can live here and in the dream world at the same time. Some of us are even aware we are dreaming when in the dream world. It's called lucid dreaming. But that's a topic for another time. What's important now is something else."

"What's that?" asked Squirrel.

"If you're lucky, the different worlds come together at just the right time and in the right way."

Squirrel opened his eyes, emerging from his memory. He missed Fire and wished he could talk to him now. But remembering Fire's words helped him feel better about leaving behind all he knew and traveling to a place he could barely imagine. He often knew he was dreaming while in the dream world. Now at least he had a word for it.

"Lucid dreaming," he whispered. He wished he could ask Fire more about how it worked.

He still didn't understand how he could live in two worlds with

32

both of them being real places—or how the two worlds could come together. But one thing he knew for sure. He didn't want to have any more dreams about storms.

Soon he would fly on one of the planes Fire had called a silver bird. That was better than dangling lifeless on a peg, lying on the dirty floor, or feeling rejected and ignored. He slid down into the pocket of the boy's backpack and tried to imagine the worlds outside the airport gift shop.

Chapter 5

A Lesson in Imagination

Of course it is happening inside your head, Harry,
but why on earth should that mean that it is not real?

—J. K. Rowling, *Harry Potter and the Deathly Hallows*

Squirrel poked his head out of the backpack's pocket, wondering how long he had been napping since remembering his conversation with Fire. Travis and his mother were sitting in seats next to the ticket counter near the boarding gate and across the corridor from the gift shop. Squirrel was able to see the puppets on the tree through the store window. A wave of sorrow washed over him. He was leaving the only life he had ever known other than his dreams. Yet he was curious about the journey he was about to take and hoped they would board their plane soon.

Outside the nearby window, a wave of dark clouds moved across the sky toward the airport, and Squirrel wondered if the plane could fly in a rainstorm. Inside, he noticed most of the seats were taken, and several people were standing near the ticket counter. Sitting in the row directly across from him, a dark-skinned girl dressed in jeans and a Seahawks jacket was eating a sandwich. Next to her, a man sprouting white hair beneath a black cowboy hat flipped through pages of a newspaper. Squirrel had seen stacks of newspapers delivered each morning to the gift shop. He and the other puppets were curious about why some people purchased them.

Several passengers stared at smartphones. Squirrel had no idea what was so fascinating about pictures in a tiny box that caused people to ignore one another. He hoped there would be enough seats on a small plane for everyone who was waiting for the flight.

Squirrel closed his eyes and imagined boarding a plane while hanging out of his boy's backpack. Perhaps, like Fire said, the dream world was as real as the sky through which he was about to fly. Then he had a curious thought. *Maybe the inside of a plane is another world.*

"Hey, Squirrel," Travis said, pulling him out of the backpack. "You didn't have a name on your tag. I'll call you Squirrel."

Squirrel was happy the boy gave him the same name as the one his puppet friends had given him. Then he felt the boy's hand slide into his paws, and he heard him say, "Squirrel, let's play. You have to use your imagination when we play." Squirrel wished Travis could hear him laugh. He had spent a lifetime imagining a life somewhere else.

When Travis inserted fingers into his puppet mouth and paws, Squirrel heard the boy's words as his own. "Here you are, Rocket Man. I found you."

Under direction of the boy's hand, he picked the bendable action figure from the backpack and set it on the empty seat next to them. Then he lifted up a package of mini cookies and put it to the side of the action figure. It felt strange having the boy control what he did with his paws and the words that came from his mouth.

"Do you want some snacks, little Squirrel?" the boy's laughing voice teased.

With his other hand, Travis pulled a worn, stuffed green frog out of the backpack and a device he called an electronic tablet. He set both the tablet and the frog on the empty seat. Squirrel thought the tablet must be a bigger version of a smartphone.

Finally, Travis lifted a plastic bag from the bottom of the backpack. Withdrawing his hand from inside Squirrel, he slid the top open. A collection of tiny plastic heroes and villains spilled onto the floor.

Travis dropped down onto the carpet and arranged the heroes and villains in neat rows, naming each one. Then he slid his hand back into Squirrel's paws and mouth, making them move as he imagined aloud adventures with different combinations of characters.

Although Squirrel had seen children play with superhero figures sold in the gift shop, he didn't know much about their magical abilities. He remembered that one superhero could fly and see through walls. He quickly learned that another could climb buildings and swing across alleys on a thread spun out of thin air. Squirrel particularly admired the heroes that could shapeshift, breathe under water, or ride on a broom while hitting a winged ball.

During the imaginary games he played with Travis, Squirrel loved how the heroes defeated the bad guys in battles by using weapons like light sabers, magic wands, infinity stones, and tesseracts. He even learned that some superheroes hid their real identities behind those of ordinary people with regular jobs. He wondered if Fire and Wings would understand the boy's characters and the different worlds where they played. They were a lot like dreams.

Squirrel wanted to be more than just an ordinary squirrel. He hoped he had a special talent that would make him a superhero. Maybe the lion had been right, and what he really needed was courage. It was the quality all the boy's heroes seemed to have in common.

"Attention, all passengers on American Airlines flight 728 to Philadelphia. Due to inclement weather, the flight is delayed."

Travis's mother put down her book and sighed. "Well, that's bad news."

Travis dropped Squirrel onto his lap, scooped up his little characters, and sealed them in the plastic bag. He stuffed the bag, Rocket Man, and the frog into the backpack. Then he stood up, pushed Squirrel into the back pocket of the backpack, and set it on the seat next to him.

Squirrel lifted his eyes over the pocket's opening. He saw Travis pick up his tablet and the package of mini cookies and sit down. Fluffing his tail and closing his eyes, Squirrel hoped to slip into another dream.

Chapter 6

Time to Fly

The moment you doubt whether you can fly,
you cease forever to be able to do it.

—J. M. Barrie, *Peter Pan*

When Squirrel entered the dream world, the first rays of dawn spilled across the dew-covered grass, creating a pattern of moving shadows. Aware he was dreaming, Squirrel shook his tail excitedly. Then he scanned the area, relieved it was not raining. Oaks and sycamores shaded the path that zigzagged through tall orange flowers. On the sunny side of the path, the familiar river meandered past exposed roots rising from muddy banks. A jewel-colored damselfly with a white spot on its wing was perched on a shiny leaf. Its jaw hung open in a lopsided grin as Squirrel noticed its ball-shaped eyes staring at him.

No longer a puppet waiting for the boy's hands to make his mouth move or guide his paws, Squirrel sniffed the fresh scents of grass and wildflowers. Bounding toward the wide trunk of the old oak tree, he had one purpose in mind: to experience this dream world as a real squirrel for as long as possible.

With renewed determination, he sunk his claws into the oak's bark like he had learned to do during past dream adventures. Then he scaled the trunk to its highest branch. After scampering the length of the branch, he leaped through the leaves to a white, mottled branch on a neighboring tree. Feeling pleased with himself, he shouted out a string of barks as his fur rippled down to the tip of his tail. "The dragon was right. This world is real, and I can fly!"

Then he recalled his last dream. He looked down and scanned the riverbanks, looking for his friends. The last thing he had seen before waking up was Roar padding across the wet lawn toward a grove of trees in the pouring rain. Bandita had waddled after him, mumbling something about leaving his dream world. Yet, while waking up from that dream, Squirrel had caught a glimpse of her pulling a cereal box from a garbage can that had blown over onto the patio of the nearby cottage.

Feeling tightness in his chest, he remembered the large white heart on the raccoon's chest fur. The other puppets always teased her about that heart. She would answer by telling them that it was a birthmark and that it meant she spoke from her heart. Perhaps that was why she had always been a friend he could trust.

Suddenly, a familiar voice broke his reverie. "Hey, Squirrel, it's a fine place you've found here."

Squirrel turned toward the hawk, who was perched on a nearby branch. A dead mouse dangled from one of his talons. "Wings, you surprised me. You're here in my dream world! And you're eating something!"

"Well, it's not a juicy, young rabbit, but it'll do for a small breakfast. I've seen a number of songbirds and furry rodents. There's more than enough food for me to survive quite well. And I've met other hawks like me here, ones with striped tails and fluffy white chest feathers. They tell me they're part of a tribe called the Cooper's Hawks."

"At least I have one friend in this place," Squirrel said, silently questioning his words.

"You could do worse than having a hawk as a friend. Let's go exploring," Wings said, pointing his wing toward an overgrown trail. "I wonder where the path in that grove of trees leads."

Squirrel scampered down the tree trunk and leaped. Before he hit the ground, he woke up.

*

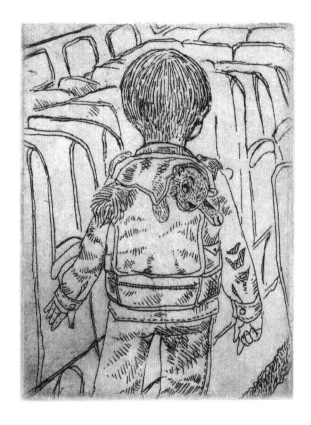

"Attention, passengers on American Airlines flight number 728 to Philadelphia. We are now boarding first-class passengers, members of the military, and those with special needs at gate C13."

Squirrel watched Travis pick up his backpack and follow his mother to the line designated for priority boarding. Then from the boy's back, he observed the crowd of frowning passengers that had formed behind them. Once they had boarded the plane, he heard Travis's mother ask Travis if he wanted the seat next to the aisle or by the window.

Travis answered quickly. "I want the aisle seat so that I can see everything that's going on inside the plane. It's cloudy outside, and I wouldn't be able to see anything once we're in the sky."

After Travis and his mother had settled in their seats, Travis pulled Squirrel out from the backpack and set him in his lap. Squirrel hoped the plane would take off soon. He imagined flying into the clouds as he had seen planes do through the window of the gift shop.

Finally, the flight attendant addressed the passengers. "Welcome aboard. The boarding door is now closed. Please set your electronic devices to airplane mode. Our flight time to Philadelphia will be approximately five hours and nine minutes."

Then the monitor popped open on the back of the seat in front of where Squirrel sat with Travis. Squirrel watched the screen with fascination as a uniformed woman talked about emergency instructions, including the location of exits, the use of oxygen masks, and how to fasten seat belts. She pointed to the spot where life vests and seat cushions were located in the unlikely event of a water landing, and then she declared smoking was not allowed. Squirrel wondered how long the instructions would last.

When the monitor closed, the flight attendant walked up and down the aisle, reminding passengers to make sure all tray tables and seat backs were in an upright position. He checked on Travis to make sure his seat belt was fastened. When the plane began to move, Squirrel held his breath. He knew the plane had lifted off the runway when he felt a bump and then a nauseating sense, he had left his stomach on the ground.

Unable to see what was happening outside the plane while in flight, Squirrel wanted to reenter the dream world, where he could fly from one tree to the next. He hoped his friends would show up again, even if in his waking life they were still in the gift shop. The sound of the plane's engine lulled Squirrel back to sleep.

Chapter 7

The Woman Wearing Purple Running Shoes

Here today, up and off to somewhere else
tomorrow! Travel, change, interest, excitement!
The whole world before you, and a
horizon that's always changing.

—Kenneth Grahame, *The Wind in the Willows*

"Hello, little squirrel. Are you lost?"

From where he stood on a grassy field, Squirrel saw only purple running shoes. One of the laces was untied. He glanced up just as an older woman bent down level with his face, her eyes meeting his. Beneath a floppy red hat, her gray eyes sparkled with playfulness, and her mostly white hair blossomed around her flushed face. He had seen women like her in the gift shop. They were called grandmothers, and they often admired the animals on the puppet tree, exclaiming how realistic they were. Squirrel had never seen a human in the dream world until now. Maybe she was someone's grandmother.

"I've been collecting four-leaf clovers," she said, clutching a fistful in her wrinkled hand. "Oh, but I bet you're not interested in clover. I have a bag of peanuts and other snacks on the bench where

I'm planning to have lunch. Come along, and I'll share my treats with you."

Squirrel was curious about the woman. He watched her stuff the clover into a pocket of a billowing, flowered skirt as he followed her across the field to a gravel road. An old iron bench stood in a patch of tiny yellow flowers next to the road. Clusters of thick bushes with white flowers lined the opposite side of the road. Black, orange, and white patterned butterflies fluttered from one bloom to another.

Sitting down on the bench, the woman unfolded her bag of treats as Squirrel crouched on the ground watching her. "My goodness," she said with a wide smile. "There's been a lot of rain recently, and the entire hollow is overgrown. And look at all the monarch butterflies. There are four generations of them each summer. Soon the leaves will turn from green to shades of yellow, orange, and red. And then the fourth generation of these remarkable butterflies will migrate to Mexico for the winter."

Squirrel didn't know much about butterflies. But he had once seen a book about them in the gift shop, and there had been a stuffed one on the puppet tree. He had heard a clerk tell a customer that its name was Monarch.

While he watched the butterflies hover over the bushes next to the road, Squirrel's nose began to twitch. He ran to the bushes and sniffed, wondering if the flowers were good to eat. The flowers had a sweet scent like the candles that had been on a table next to the puppet tree.

"No, no, little squirrel, not those bushes!" the woman yelled. "They're Asian honeysuckle, invasive plants for this part of the country. Not good for our native birds and animals. I keep trying to cut them back. You'll like peanuts much better than those flowers."

Squirrel scampered back to where the woman sat on the bench. He had never before in his dreams thought so much about eating. He stood up and rubbed his paw over an aching stomach.

Holding a peanut between two fingers, the woman cracked the shell and laid two small nuts on the ground. Squirrel snatched up one nut. Grasping it in his forepaws, he sat down on his back legs and began to chew. He quickly finished it and picked up the second one. The woman continued to feed him delicious snacks, things she called sunflower seeds and popcorn.

"I want to live here forever," Squirrel chittered.

"What a happy squirrel you are," the woman said as her rosy cheeks glistened in the sunlight. Then her voice softened. "You know, this is a special place. It's a wildlife sanctuary, right here on the White River. I call it Riverwood Hollow."

Now Squirrel's dream world had a name. Wanting to hear more, Squirrel jumped up onto the bench and sat next to the woman. During his stay in the gift shop, he had learned human language better than the other puppets. Although the woman talked about things that were unfamiliar to him, he understood her words. Perking his ears, he placed his two paws in the middle of his chest and eagerly waited for what the woman would say next.

"Riverwood Hollow is the home of a mystical forest. It is surrounded by the spirits of enchanted trees: hickories, oaks, and sycamores, and even an ash or two that survived the recent blight known as the Emerald Ash Borer. It's been a terrible plight that's affected many ash trees here in the Midwest." The woman paused and pointed to the area at the end of the road. "Little squirrel, look beyond this field. Do you see that pond?"

Squirrel turned around so that he could see the pond. He spotted a large blue-gray bird with a snake-like neck and long legs wading through the water. The surface was covered with wide green leaves. He remembered a bird on the puppet tree called Great Blue One. The shop manager had said it was a blue heron when she opened one of the shipments. Great Blue One sold on the first day he arrived. Squirrel picked up another salty peanut and devoured it within seconds. He wondered about other creatures that might live in Riverwood Hollow.

"Everything here is magical," the woman continued. "There are worlds within worlds, ones that are visible only to those who can see them. At the end of that path of thorny honeysuckle bushes to the right of the pond, there's a maze where lichen-covered pebbles lie half-buried in sandy soil. During late spring days, turtles dig nests and lay their eggs there."

The woman paused, lowering her voice as though she was about to tell him something important. "And would you like to know about the magic mailbox in Riverwood Hollow?"

He nodded his head, flicking his tail back and forth. "I'm a real squirrel, and this is a real place!" he barked.

*

Squirrel woke up in the boy's arms as a cold hand touch his head. "That's not a real squirrel, is it?" the flight attendant asked.

"No, but he's real to me!" Travis asserted, holding the squirrel against his shoulder as his mother shoved his backpack beneath the seat in front of him. "He's my puppet named Squirrel. I've added him to my collection of superheroes. I like to create make-believe stories and write them for my class assignments in school."

"Well then, I won't have to remove him from the cabin," the flight attendant replied, chuckling in a way that Squirrel knew he was amused.

"Can I hold him?" Travis asked. "I don't think he wants to sleep in my backpack on the floor."

"Of course, keep him in your lap. But don't let me catch him scurrying among the other passengers." The flight attendant smiled at Travis's mother. "I hope you both enjoy flying first class today."

"I am grateful," she said, brushing loose strands of hair off her cheeks. "It's been a rough start this morning. We're traveling to Indianapolis to my mother-in-law's home for Christmas. It's really strange flying over Indianapolis all the way east to Philadelphia and then taking another plane, flying back west to Indianapolis. But it was the only flight itinerary I could book during this busy holiday season. My name is Anne, and this is Travis."

"My name's Karl," the flight attendant said. "I will do everything I can to make your trip enjoyable. The weather doesn't look good in Philadelphia for connections. There's a huge snowstorm moving over the entire Midwest. There may be a large number of delays and cancellations this week. Most likely, it's going to be a longer trip than expected."

"Thank you so much for your kindness. I heard on the news before boarding that it's the largest blizzard to hit in the past twenty years."

Karl nodded. "I'll be serving beverages and lunch as soon as we reach our flight's cruising altitude. In the meantime, here are a couple of blankets and headphones—and a cookie for Travis and a package of peanuts for the squirrel." Karl paused, turning to Travis. "We have a marvelous film, *The Grinch,* you and your friend might enjoy on this flight. It's an older one, but kids your age love it."

From his place near Travis's shoulder, Squirrel watched Karl move down the aisle toward the seats in front of him. There was a bag on the floor that was partially spilling into the aisle. When Karl stooped to pick up the bag, his pants lifted up from his shoes. The flight attendant wore purple socks.

Chapter 8

Letter to Dad

Nothing is hopeless: We must hope for everything.

—Madeleine L'Engle, Mrs. Who, quoting
Euripides, *A Wrinkle in Time*

Travis wasn't interested in seeing *The Grinch*. He had already seen it three times. He wanted to talk to his mother about something that had been on his mind since they had left home without his father. He set the cookie on the tray attached to the seat in front of him. Then he took a large gulp of soda from the bottle his mother had purchased from the airport snack bar.

Turning toward his mother, he asked the question that had been troubling him. "Mom, how come Daddy isn't coming with us for Christmas this year?"

Anne closed the book she had been reading and put her arm around his shoulder. "He says he has too much work to finish. There's a policy with his law firm about billable hours."

Travis noticed his mother's expression as she pursed her lips. He knew she really didn't want to discuss the subject. But he continued to press her for more information. "What does *billable hours* mean?"

Anne cleared her throat. "Your dad has to work a lot of hours for the clients he helps. That way, he makes money for his firm, and then they are able to pay him a good salary."

"I still don't understand. I wish he could be here with us. I know his job as a lawyer is important. But it's Christmas, and most of my friends have fathers who don't work all the time. It seems like he's never home."

"Travis, your father wants to provide the best for us. He has dreams for your future that include special experiences, summer camps, trips, and eventually college. He wants you to have the life he never had for himself after his father died."

"How old was he when his father died?"

"He was about your age. It was tough for him growing up without the things other kids had in their lives."

"I just want my dad to be with me more often—you know, like the dads who take their kids to basketball games, the movies, and on vacations to the beach. Now when he comes home, I'm already asleep in bed."

"I know. But he loves you very much."

"I love him too," Travis murmured as he turned his face back toward the aisle. He didn't want his mother to see the tears forming in his eyes. He always tried to hide his sadness about missing his dad from his mother.

"Hey, I have an idea," Anne said. "I brought a couple of Christmas cards, and they're in my tote bag. Why don't you write him a note? We can mail it as soon as we see a mailbox."

Travis turned toward his mother and squeezed out a reply. "Couldn't we just email him or text him?"

"Yes, we'll message or call him later, but it's not the same thing. A letter written by hand is much better, more personal." Anne pulled her bag out from beneath her seat. She reached inside and pulled out a shiny card decorated with silver glitter. "Here's a nice one with a family standing next to a decorated Christmas tree. I have a pen for you to use."

"But what do I write in my letter?"

"Just tell him how you feel. That you miss him and love him. I can help you with the right words, if you'd like."

Travis pushed aside the cookie and soda and placed the card on the tray in front of him. Without his mother's help, he printed the words that came to him easily.

Dear Dad,
We are flying on a big airplane, just like the
airplane model Santa Claus gave me last Christmas.
It would be so much fun
if you were with us. I miss you, and Mom does too.
I love you.
Travis.

Travis slid the card into the envelope and handed it to his mother. He watched as she wiped a tear from her cheek and reached into her bag, pulling out her wallet. She retrieved a stamp and affixed it to the envelope. Then she handed the envelope back to Travis and helped him print his dad's name and the address of his law office on the front. Travis continued to hold the envelope in his hand as he pulled Squirrel out from the seat where he had slipped down next to the armrest.

As the flight attendant moved down the aisle and picked up the empty cookie package and soda bottle, Travis closed his eyes. He remembered how his father had always bought him the latest toys. But now the toys didn't matter as much. He just wanted to have more time with his father.

"I hope the letter will reach him before Christmas," he whispered like a prayer. He fell asleep still holding the letter in his hand.

Chapter 9

The Magic Mailbox

And above all, watch with glittering
eyes the whole world around you
because the greatest secrets are always
hidden in the most unlikely places.
Those who don't believe in magic will never find it.

—Roald Dahl, *The Minpins*

Travis pushed his way through the trees that formed a tunnel over a barely visible path. The branches were thick with green leaves, and only a thin stream of speckled sunlight penetrated their cover. Stepping over a fallen log, Travis trekked forward, kicking his feet through a layer of mulch. The odor reminded him of his mother's spring flower garden.

Eventually, the tunnel opened onto a gravel road. A row of flowering bushes bordered the road on the right. To the left, a meadow carpeted with clover and yellow wildflowers stretched toward a pond in the distance. Birds chirped and trilled from treetops, and chipmunks scampered around a rusted bench near a fire ring. Travis blinked. The entire meadow was swarming with dragonflies. He heard water splashing from beyond a line of trees that towered over the left side of the meadow.

After Travis walked a short distance along the road, he came to a spot where two footpaths split off from the road. One path spiraled around the right side of the pond before disappearing into overgrown bushes and majestic trees. The second path circled around the left side of the pond. The gravel road made a sharp left turn and led to a concrete boat ramp that descended into murky water.

At this intersection, Travis approached a metal mailbox mounted on a wood post. It looked like the mailboxes he had seen lining the curbs in front of houses where he lived. "A funny place to put a mailbox, with no houses nearby," he said.

"Yes indeed," replied a cheerful voice.

Travis turned, staring down at purple running shoes. An old woman with puffy white hair was bent over, moving her hands through the grass as though searching for something.

"Have you lost something?" he asked, curious about her strange behavior.

The woman stood up, waving a handful of clover. Her flushed face framed gray eyes and a kindhearted smile. "I'm looking for four-leaf clovers. I always find them here, most of the time more than one. They keep popping out of the ground everywhere I walk. It's a magic place, just like this mailbox."

"So, can I mail a letter here?" Travis asked.

"Absolutely. You can write a letter to anyone and put it in this box. It will be delivered. But your intention must be clear, and you must address the envelope to the exact address for the person to whom you wish it to be sent."

Travis felt his jaw tighten with determination. "I want to mail a very important letter to my father. It's already addressed and in an envelope with a stamp. Is that possible?"

"Certainly," the old woman replied.

"Are you sure the mail person knows about this box? It's out in the middle of nowhere."

Travis was about to ask another question when the woman continued. "I said the mailbox was magic, and so it is. It also delivers mail. What is it that you most need right now for your adventure?"

"Well ... I ... ah," Travis began. Then, biting his lip, he realized the squirrel puppet was no longer in his arms. He turned in a circle, searching the area near the gravel road. "I've lost Squirrel ... my ... my new friend. I was just holding him, and now he's gone!"

The woman pointed to the strap on his shoulder holding the backpack. "What about your backpack?"

Travis dropped the backpack to the ground, bent over, and searched every compartment. There were cookies, a bendable action figure, a plastic bag of superheroes, an electronic tablet, and a stuffed frog at the bottom of the bag. But the squirrel was missing from the pocket where he normally kept him. "He's gone! I've got to find him."

The woman stuffed a four-leaf clover into the pocket of her skirt before speaking. "Squirrels can be pretty tricky when scampering through the woods. Sometimes they sit on a tree branch and bark or chatter. They climb the tree higher than anyone can see and leap to a branch on another tree. Then they run off somewhere. You don't want to get lost searching for him. Maybe a map of this place would help."

"Yeah, I guess I could use a map," Travis said, picking up his backpack from the ground.

"Why don't you check inside the mailbox? The red flag is raised. You know what that means, don't you? It means there's something in the box that needs to be picked up."

Travis scratched his head. "But won't it be something for the mail person to pick up and deliver somewhere else?"

"Not necessarily," the old woman said. "Sometimes this mailbox has something for the person who is standing near it. Something a boy might need. Like I said, it's a magic mailbox."

Travis took a breath and walked toward the box. Pulling down the latch, he reached inside and withdrew a folded piece of thick, yellowed paper. He turned it over and read aloud, "Riverwood Hollow."

"Yes, my dear boy. That's the name of this place."

Travis unfolded the paper. "It looks like a map," he said. "And there's something written beneath the map."

The woman's eyes sparkled in the sunlight. "Perhaps some instructions."

Travis studied the words and began to read the message aloud. "To the person who needs this map, it offers its service freely. But beware of where it might take you." He paused for a moment. Then, feeling curious, he asked, "What do the words mean?"

"It means the map will help you. But you should be careful, for there could be surprises or even dangers," the woman answered.

Travis suddenly saw additional words that had not been there when he first looked at the map. "There's more. Adventures are for cour … age … ous souls," he said, pronouncing the word.

The woman smiled. "Courageous souls. It means very brave."

"Courageous seems like a bigger word than brave. I don't know for sure if I'm brave or courageous."

"Courage is a quality one has when doing something for love," the woman said as she touched the top of Travis's head.

"Well, I love my dad and want to mail the letter I wrote to him. And I love Squirrel, so I'll do what I can to find him."

"And so, my dear, you are both brave and courageous."

Travis realized that he was still holding the letter to his father in his hands, along with the map. "What about my letter? Can I really mail it here?"

"Yes, of course you can. Where there's love, you'll find big magic, especially by way of this mailbox."

Travis set the map on top of the mailbox and pulled down the latch on the door. He slid the letter onto a vacant shelf, hoping the old woman was right about the box being magic.

"You might need a bit of luck," the woman said. She reached into her pocket and pulled out a four-leaf clover. "Just for you."

Travis took the four-leaf clover from the woman's outstretched hand and pushed it into the pocket of his jeans.

*

When Travis awoke, he reached into the pocket of his pants. Deep beneath a candy wrapper, he felt it. The four-leaf clover. He found Squirrel next to him in his airplane seat. He searched for the map and then remembered he had left it on top of the mailbox.

"I wonder if a person can be in a dream and in real life at the same time," Travis mumbled under his breath.

"Travis, you were talking in your sleep, and you missed lunch," his mother said, touching his shoulder.

"Mom, I was having the coolest dream about a magic mailbox. It felt so real."

"Some dreams are like that. I—" His mother began when the voice of the flight attendant interrupted her words.

"Attention, all passengers. We are making our final approach to the Philadelphia International Airport. Please return your seats to the upright position and the tray tables to their storage space. We will be landing at gate B6 in fifteen minutes. Remember to check the monitors or your American Airlines app for connections and departures. There are several delays and cancellations due to the unexpected severity of the snowstorm moving across the Midwest."

"Mom," Travis said, tapping her shoulder, "why do people dream? And where do they go in their dreams?"

"Travis, we have to get ready for landing. That conversation is an important one that will take some time. We'll talk later. Let's get your coat back on. The weather is going to be colder here than in Seattle. And we must hurry to our next flight. It is scheduled to take off soon."

"You mean if it hasn't been delayed," Travis said, pushing Squirrel back into the top of his backpack.

Chapter 10

Delayed, Canceled, Standby

So many miracles have not yet happened.

—Kate DiCamillo, *Flora & Ulysses:*
The Illuminated Adventures

Squirrel peered over the top pocket of the backpack as Travis and his mother gathered up their carry-on bags. When they moved into the aisle behind other passengers, Squirrel figured they would be exiting the plane. He had been listening to the conversations between Travis and his mother and heard the sadness in the boy's words about missing his father. Squirrel missed his friends at the gift shop, so he understood the boy's feelings. He wondered what it was like to have parents who said those magic words, *I love you.* Words that made his chest ache.

Stuffed into a small space, he tried to reposition his body, but only his tail shifted slightly. Attempts to move without human hands in the waking world caused him frustration, especially after experiencing the freedom of being a real squirrel in Riverwood Hollow.

After they made their way into the terminal, Anne stopped, pointing to something Squirrel couldn't see from his place in the backpack. "There are the monitors that list the departing and arriving flights," she said. "We can check the status of our flight."

"I see our flight number," Travis said. "It is departing in terminal C, at gate eighteen, but it's been delayed.

"We have more time than I thought," Anne said. "We're in terminal B, so we'll need to walk down the concourse to terminal C. After we find our gate, maybe we can do a bit of shopping and grab a bite to eat."

Riding in the backpack past shops and restaurants, Squirrel sat in the perfect spot to observe people browsing around brightly lit stores filled with knickknacks, food items, magazines, and books. He watched frowning passengers dragging bags on rollers and people lining up at snack bars. He became too curious about things happening in the terminal to think about love, sadness, or being stuck in a backpack.

Finally, they arrived at the gate for the flight to Indianapolis. Squirrel heard Anne exhale in relief. "Whew, the flight has been delayed even longer," she said. "The departure time has been moved to 8:05 p.m."

Just as Squirrel had become comfortable with the new surroundings, a voice blared from the sound system. "Attention, passengers of American Airlines flight 4495 scheduled to depart at 8:05 p.m. to Indianapolis. The flight has been canceled due to the blizzard. Please proceed to one of the nearest agents to reschedule your flight."

Squirrel remembered the conversation about the big snowstorm, but he had never seen snow. Considering the way things had been going while traveling through a blizzard, he wasn't interested in seeing snow in the future.

After locating an American Airlines information counter, Travis followed his mother first in line of grumbling passengers. When he set his backpack on the counter, Squirrel watched the conversation with growing interest. Anne leaned toward an agent with long black hair as she set two tickets on the counter.

The agent picked up the tickets and gave them a quick glance. "Oh, Indianapolis," she said with a grimace. Her expression reminded Squirrel of ones he had seen on shoppers in the gift shop when they couldn't make a decision about a purchase. Pushing her glasses up the bridge of her nose, the agent turned toward the computer keyboard and began typing.

After a few minutes, she looked up from her computer. "If you go now to gate F14, there's another flight. It's American Airlines Eagle flight 4453, departing at 8:45 p.m. You can fly standby. But I have to warn you, everything is backed up this evening. Even that flight was delayed, and most likely it'll also be canceled."

"Travis, let's go," Anne said. "That gate is on the other side of the airport, so we have to go to a different terminal."

Fifteen minutes later, they stood behind other passengers in another line. Travis pulled Squirrel out of the backpack and held him in his arms. Squirrel smiled, pleased he could watch things more easily. When they reached the counter, Anne presented their tickets to the agent, whose hands snatched them while his eyes stayed focused on the computer screen.

"I'm so sorry, but this flight has been canceled," the agent said, his brown eyes moving between Anne and the computer screen

"What? This flight is canceled too?" Anne said. "I should have guessed."

"The blizzard is a problem for all the flights in and out of the Midwest. I'll try to book you on one of tomorrow morning's flights." The agent paused his typing and stared intently at the computer screen. Then typing again, he groaned. "Oh! I see you have first-class tickets. Everything is booked on tomorrow's flights, but perhaps something will open up. Let me see what I can do."

Anne pointed to Squirrel. "It's all his fault. That squirrel is a trickster for sure!" she declared with a silly grin. Noticing the gleam in her eyes, Squirrel was reminded of Roar when he teased the other puppets.

The agent glanced up from the keyboard. Raising his eyebrows, he bit his lip before returning to his typing.

"Mom, it's not Squirrel's fault about the weather," Travis said.

"I'm so sorry, Travis," his mother said. "I'm just making a joke to lighten this situation. Some people think squirrels are trickster animals like foxes. I have a friend who believes that trickster animals can cause mischief or a change in plans."

The agent continued to type on the computer keyboard. But Squirrel noticed him arching his eyebrows again after Anne's comments. Then he heard passengers in the line behind them grumbling about missing holiday events with their families.

Drumming her fingers on the counter, Anne continued talking to Travis. "Your squirrel puppet is a type of squirrel we call a fox squirrel back in Indiana where I grew up. His tail is as big as his body, and it's bushy and red like a fox's tail. When I was a girl, we all knew squirrels were tricky creatures."

Hearing Anne's descriptions, Squirrel wanted to chitter and flick his tail. Instead, he thought, *I bet the boy's mother would be waving her tail around ... if she had one.*

The agent looked up and shook his head. "The best I can do is offer you two tickets for standby seats on tomorrow morning's flight 4198, departing at 10:40 a.m. It's a direct flight to Indianapolis. But it's possible that all the flights will be overbooked for tomorrow, so you may have to fly standby for more than one flight."

"What about a hotel room for my son and me tonight? Can that be arranged?"

"Yes, of course," the agent replied. Picking up a pen in one hand, he lifted a phone to his ear with his other hand. A few moments later, he handed Anne a slip of paper. "Here's a reservation confirmation for one night at the Sheraton Airport Suites Hotel."

"Whew, I'll be glad to have a nice place to stay," Anne said. "Thank you so much for your help. It must be terribly difficult for airline employees who are helping so many stranded passengers during a holiday season."

The agent rubbed his eyes. "This is the biggest storm I've ever seen affecting the airport. The holidays have added more stress to the situation. You can catch the shuttle bus to your hotel in zone 4. All the terminals have a zone 4. Just follow the signs to ground transportation. Your bus will have the name of the hotel printed on the side. You won't need to call for pickup. All the shuttles pick up passengers every half hour during this time of the day."

"Thank you again," Anne said, taking Travis's hand.

A half hour later, they exited the airport and stood on the curb in freezing sleet, waiting for the hotel shuttle. Travis stuffed Squirrel back into the pocket of the backpack. Having felt the blast of cold air, Squirrel worried about what would happen next.

Chapter 11

A Princely Friend

Misfortune tests the sincerity of friendship.

—Aesop, *The Bear and the Travelers*

Squirrel dropped into a cluster of bushes filled with red berries. He knew he was in his dream world again. Climbing over exposed roots and fallen logs, he threaded his way through a dense undergrowth of twisting branches. He eventually made his way into the field of clover where he once met an old woman who fed him handfuls of tasty treats. He stood up and placed his paws on his chest, surveying the area. Tall trees shaded small saplings growing near the bank of the pond. A sandy path skirted around the pond that led into a wide patch of marsh grass. He dashed toward the pond.

Curious about what was on the other side of the pond, he followed the path to the marsh grass. When he came to a fallen log shaded by a split-trunked tree, he stopped. Rows of small fan-like shapes sprouted from the side of the log untouched by the sunlight. Curious, he sniffed, then touched the strange shapes. They felt like the rubber duck toy that had been placed in his paws when he was featured in one of the gift shop's displays.

"Hey, little squirrel, you don't want to eat those. Mushrooms can be deadly."

Startled by the voice, Squirrel scampered behind the tree and climbed up the trunk to a safe distance from the forest floor. Then he looked down and searched for the source of the voice. A huge rust-colored squirrel stood upright on two legs, raising a paw in his direction. Frightened by the appearance of a larger version of himself, Squirrel scurried farther up the tree and crept out onto a thin branch. He heard the limb snap just before plummeting into a shallow hole covered with broken shells. Kicking away the shells, he picked himself up and ran to another tree.

Pausing at the trunk and glancing back toward the hole, he expected to see the other squirrel following him. Instead, he saw a huge black animal racing down the path. Its pointed teeth dripped foaming moisture from a panting jaw. The animal was headed in his direction. It took Squirrel precious moments to determine that the animal was a dog like one of the puppets that once hung on a peg near him in the gift shop.

Squirrel whipped his tail back and forth, hoping to scare off the dog. Then, confused about where to find a hiding place, he darted this way and that, racing through the sandy grassland. Spotting trees with peeling bark, he ran in their direction. The dog was closing in behind him. Never in his life as a puppet had he been required to run and never this fast in his dreams. Now he flew ahead of the snarling dog on a path that wasn't really much of a path. Broken tree limbs blocked escape routes to most of the trees. He had no idea which way to turn.

"This way, numnuts!"

He turned to his right just as the large squirrel shoved him toward the trunk of one of the trees with peeling bark. At this point, he had no choice but to trust the other squirrel, who was doing something very strange. While racing around the trunk of the tree, he was flicking his spiked tail up and down and chattering viciously at the approaching dog.

"Climb this sycamore tree now!" the big squirrel yelled.

The big squirrel's high-pitched barks and tail waving provided the needed distraction for Squirrel to scramble up the tree. Once out of reach of the dog, he settled into a hollow space where the trunk split into two branches. The big squirrel quickly joined him, still waving his inflated tail.

Relieved to be in a safe place, Squirrel watched the dog leap up and down, howling in frenzied attempts to reach them. Then Squirrel copied the big squirrel's behavior, taunting the dog by flicking his tail and barking screechy insults. He felt excited by the turn of events that enabled him to provoke the dog's frustration.

Finally, the dog tired and ran back down the path, and Squirrel had the opportunity to study the animal who had helped him. Other than being much larger, the big squirrel had a giant tail that was nearly twice the size of Squirrel's tail when it was inflated. He smelled different, like the floor around the puppet tree where kids sometimes tracked in dirt on their shoes. And his face was more confident and rugged looking, as though he had never seen the inside of a gift shop.

Satisfied that the big squirrel was a friend rather than an enemy, Squirrel looked at him directly. "Who's that nasty dog?" he asked.

The big squirrel chuckled. "His name is Brutus, and he comes here often, walking the path with his owner. Most of the time, he runs loose and terrorizes the inhabitants of the forest. By the way, my name's Baldwin. It means *princely friend.* And yours, little one?"

"My friends just call me Squirrel. I still need a real—"

A familiar voice interrupted his answer. "Are you OK, Squirrel?"

Squirrel looked around with surprise. It took him several moments to locate the source of the question. Then he looked up. Wings was perched on the branch above them. "Wings, what are you doing here? Did you see that dog?"

Wings pecked at his wing feathers and then nodded his head. "That dog's fangs would have torn you apart if your new friend had not rescued you. Talk about lucky. It was a good thing I happened to be flying overhead. I might not have found you."

Baldwin winced. "A hawk is your friend?"

"Yes. He's one of them," Squirrel asserted. He felt proud he had something special to brag about to Baldwin.

Baldwin gasped. "I've never seen a hawk that big. He's a monster of a bird. Aren't you afraid he'll sweep you up in his sharp talons and rip into you for his next meal?"

"What? Wings? No way. We're like family," Squirrel said. "Just a couple days ago, we were both stuffed animal puppets hanging on a puppet tree in another world. But it's really weird. I don't remember him being this large when he was a puppet."

Baldwin barked a laugh. "Well, neither of you are stuffed animals here. In this forest, your so-called friend, Wings, is a real hawk. And that changes the rules of the game."

Wings dropped onto a branch directly across from the two squirrels and peered over a hook-shaped beak directly at Squirrel. Turning his feathered head toward Baldwin, Wings stared at the big squirrel with a one-eyed look of scrutiny Squirrel recognized.

"I don't eat my friends. Besides, I suspect Squirrel's too tough to digest. However, perhaps a larger animal of the same species would be tender and moist."

Squirrel understood the hawk's intended warning in his humorous words. Though he still trusted Wings, Squirrel knew he needed to say something in support of Baldwin. "Wings, this other squirrel's name is Baldwin. Remember how he saved my life from that black dog?"

"That's right," Wings replied, widening his eyes. "How short-sighted of me to forget."

Baldwin stood up on his hind legs and extended his quivering front paws toward the hawk. "Pleased to meet you, Wings," he said. "Oh, and by the way, there's a rule here in the hollow. It's not permissible to eat those whose names you know."

Wings fluffed his speckled white chest feathers and turned his head, looking straight at Baldwin with both eyes. "Enough said about tasty meals. I've got news. I've been keeping an eye on things in this dream world of yours, Squirrel. The boy who bought you in the gift shop has been here. And he mailed a letter to his dad in the mailbox at the edge of the woods near the pond."

"Travis is here too!" Squirrel exclaimed.

The hawk paused and adjusted his wings. "There's a crone who lives in a cottage nearby. She was helping him. She told him the mailbox was magic. Now I have to tell you. I've been a skeptic about magic, but then I never thought I would fly anywhere, much less think about eating real mice … or a succulent squirrel."

"What else do you know about Travis?" Squirrel asked, trying to ignore the obvious reference to eating Baldwin.

"Bandita and Pinkie have seen the boy, though he still doesn't know we're all here. Even Shelltin is dreaming into this world. He's hiding beneath his shell, parked near the sandy paths that spiral through the field beyond the pond. That's where you fell into broken eggs. It was a turtle's nest."

"That was a turtle's nest?" Squirrel asked, scratching his head. "I remember the purple-shoed woman telling me about turtle nests."

"Yes, that's right," Baldwin interrupted. "We call that maze of sandy paths Turtle Alley. The entire area is filled with nesting turtles during late spring."

"Listen up, Baldwin," Wings said, pointing his beak in the big squirrel's direction. "There's more I need to tell my friend about Travis."

"Quick, tell me," Squirrel demanded.

"Travis is pretty sad. Even the lion, who, by the way, is nothing more than a mangy orange cat in this world of yours, is concerned."

Squirrel laughed. "Roar? That's right. I remember seeing him in another dream. He did look like a cat. That must be a real nightmare for him."

"Of course, it is. But he still worries about our family. And the boy is part of us now. That letter had to be very important."

"I know about the letter," Squirrel said. "Travis wrote it on the plane while he was flying to his grandmother's house for Christmas. His father's too busy working to travel with them. But what can we do?"

"All the puppets are talking about the situation," Wings continued.

"But how did you guys get here?" Squirrel asked.

Wings dipped his long tail feathers over the branch and rolled his eyes. "When we were left behind in the gift shop, we all decided to follow you into your dream world. Then one night when it was dark in the store, we all closed our eyes and made a group intention to be with you. We simply journeyed together into this world."

Wings paused, glancing at Baldwin. "When I told the rest of the puppets about the boy's father, we all understood the importance of being with family. But when we arrived here, something strange happened. We saw a huge dragonfly."

"Fire! He's here too!" Squirrel exclaimed.

"I said dragonfly not a dragon flying, though that's part of the story," Wings said. "We all know from our time in the gift shop that miracles happen around Christmastime. So, Fire the dragon—"

"I've seen a strange dragonfly, much bigger than the rest," Baldwin interrupted again. "Did you know that dragonflies used to be water bugs that crawled around in the muck at the bottom of that pond?"

Wings lifted his right talon toward his chest and let it fall again. "Listen here, Baldwin. I still need to talk to Squirrel about his boy."

"Where is he? Is he safe?" Squirrel asked. With these words, Squirrel felt the touch of Travis's hand, and the dream world faded.

Chapter 12

If It Were My Dream

Our children remind us ... that we do not have to go
to sleep in order to dream and that when we imagine
something vividly ... we may be punching a hole
in the world, opening a path into a larger reality.

—Robert Moss, *Dreaming True*

"We're here, Squirrel. Safe and sound in a nice hotel," Travis said, pulling him out of the backpack. "Your fur is all messed up. I bet you've been in a quarrel with my action figure."

When Squirrel saw the hotel room and the big bed where he and Travis would sleep, he wanted to jump out of the boy's hands onto the white comforter. He knew that humans slept in beds from the stories he had heard from shoppers around the puppet tree, and he'd seen a picture of one in a book. But he had never been close to a real bed. He wondered if sleeping in a nice bed would help him have better dreams. *Oh, what an adventure this will be.*

Before Squirrel could try out the bed, Anne suggested they go to the hotel restaurant for dinner. Travis lifted Squirrel from the backpack. "I think Squirrel wants to go too."

*

After the server had seated them in a brown leather booth, Travis set Squirrel in the middle of the table. "It's time to eat. You can be a part of our conversation too."

Squirrel scanned the restaurant, wondering if he might be able to eat something in this world. Most likely, it would be impossible unless the boy made his mouth move and fed him. Even then, he doubted he could taste or swallow anything. At least he wasn't buried in a backpack and could watch things happening and listen to the conversation.

When the server returned to take their orders, she set two glasses of water and a bowl of mixed nuts on the table. "I don't see this every day, a squirrel in our hotel," she said. "But I thought your traveling pet might like a snack."

Anne smiled and thanked the server. "It's been a long day, and I'm grateful for your kindness."

The server brushed a stray gray hair from her glistening forehead. "It might help to think of all the delays and cancellations as nothing more than a dream," she said with a smile.

Anne laughed. "Or a nightmare. What would you suggest from the menu?"

"Our chicken fingers are extra crispy, so the young man will love them. For you, a bowl of homemade chicken vegetable soup. We've taken care of the squirrel."

"That would be perfect," Anne said. "I'd also like a small chef salad. And after dinner, chocolate ice-cream sundaes for both of us."

While waiting for their meals, Travis said, "Mom, do you ever have dreams when you sleep?"

"Why, yes, Travis. We all dream, though many people say they don't remember having dreams, especially adults."

Listening to the conversation, Squirrel wished he could tell Travis and his mother about his dreams. Most of all, he wished he could dip his head into the bowl of nuts on the table in front of him. He remembered the old woman, her cheerful voice, and the nuts she fed him.

"I've been having dreams," Travis said. "Sometimes they're really weird. The last dream I had while we were flying on the airplane was in a really cool place. There was an old lady there. She wore purple running shoes. And out in the middle of a field, there was a magic mailbox."

Anne leaned over the table. "That sounds like fun. Tell me more."

"The place was near water, maybe a river. There were lots of trees. Some of them were really tall, and they had white and brown spotted trunks and branches. Some of the bark was peeling off in strips."

"What a marvelous place to visit in a dream," Anne said. "Can you tell me what happened in your dream? Why don't you close your eyes and pretend you're back there now. Then tell the story like you're living it. It will be like reentering your dream."

Travis squeezed his eyes closed, frowned, and took a deep breath.

"Take your time," his mother said. "Just relax and imagine the place as you remember it."

Travis sat quietly. Squirrel watched and listened, wondering if Travis would describe the same place he had been when he met the old lady and Baldwin.

"There's a path that goes through a tunnel of tree branches,"

Travis began. "In my dream, I walk through the tunnel, and I come out on a gravel road that curves along thorny bushes on my right side and a field of flowers and clover on my left. I turn to the right. I see those tall trees with the whitish bark behind the bushes. There're lots of dragonflies too. Now that I think about it, I remember seeing one that was really large, more like a bird or a small dragon. I forgot about seeing that one until I started telling you about the dream."

Anne smiled. "I think I know of a real place just like your dream. What else happens in your dream?"

Travis took another big breath and exhaled. "I meet an old woman who's wearing purple athletic shoes. She has white hair. She's collecting four-leaf clovers, and she gives me one." He paused, reaching into the pocket of his jeans. "I thought I had it when I woke up on the plane, but it isn't there anymore."

"You must feel like your dream really happened."

"Yeah, but there's even more that happened before getting the clover." Travis closed his eyes again. "I find a magic mailbox. The lady tells me that I can mail my dad's letter, and it will be delivered. But I discover Squirrel is missing. The woman tells me that a map might help me find him. When I open the door to the mailbox, I find a map of a place called Riverwood Hollow. I pull it out of the box and unfold it. It says something strange."

"What does it say?"

"I can't quite remember. Something about being beware of where it might lead me. Then words about being courageous or brave."

Anne bit her lip. "That sounds very mysterious. What happens next?"

Squirrel felt Travis stroking his head. "I put the map on top of the box and put the letter to Dad in the box. I had the letter in my hand when I fell asleep on the plane. That's all I remember other than the woman handing me the four-leaf clover. Hey, what happened to my letter?"

"Travis, I have an idea about how it was mailed. First, tell me how you feel about your dream."

"I felt really happy when I woke up, at least about most of the dream. Now I feel curious about it all."

"And what else do you want to know about the dream other than what happened to your letter?"

"I feel really confused about the letter. That's the most important part of the dream. But I also wonder if Riverwood Hollow is a real place and if there is really such a thing as a magic mailbox."

Anne reached across the table and touched his arm. "Honey, that is such a beautiful dream. First of all, if it were my dream, I might think the tall trees with the peeling bark are sycamores, just like the trees around your grandmother's cottage on the river. I might also believe that magic mailbox could be real after all. While you were asleep on the plane, the nice flight attendant saw the letter on the floor and picked it up. When I told him how important it was, he offered to send it the most direct way possible. He said he knew about a magic mailbox where it could be mailed. That is the last time I saw the letter. Maybe it got to the magic mailbox in your dream after all."

"Mom, do you really think so?"

"Yes, I certainly think it's possible. Where there's love, there's magic, even miracles, especially at Christmastime."

Squirrel twitched his nose. Hearing the words about love, he remembered the old woman who talked about magical Riverwood Hollow. He wished he could talk to Travis and his mother.

"Wait a minute, Mom. There are a couple more things I'm curious about. After I woke up, Squirrel was in the seat next to me, and the clover was in my pocket. But now I don't have it. And I don't have the map because I left it on top of the mailbox."

"Travis, have you ever hunted for four-leaf clovers?" Anne asked. "I mean in your waking life, perhaps at school on the playground?"

"No, I once heard they mean good luck, but I've never looked for them," Travis replied. "I just wonder how the one given to me disappeared when I had it in my pocket. And I wonder if the dream really happened. It felt so real."

"If your dream were my dream," Anne said, pausing to push her hair behind her ears, "I am thinking about a wooded sanctuary next to your grandmother's cottage in Indianapolis. It's at the end of a path that winds along the White River. When I first married your father, your grandmother took me into that sanctuary, and we collected four-leaf clovers together. She always had a knack for finding them, lots of them. You haven't lost Squirrel in waking life. So, if your dream were mine, I might believe that he was off on his own adventures when you were in Riverwood Hollow."

"Could that be true? Do you think we could have adventures together in that world?"

"Yes, I think you could. Your dream world sounds wonderful. I bet you could create a story about what happens there, and you might draw some pictures too. Can you give your dream a title?"

Travis licked his lip and smiled. "I think it I will call it 'The Magic World of Riverwood Hollow.' It could be the name of the story I write."

"Your grandmother once told me that sometimes dreams are experiences of traveling to other places. When we wake up, we remember only some of what happens in our dreams. When we try to talk about them, we don't get all the facts just right. She used to say that in our dreams, we have adventures with friends, animals, magical creatures, and sometimes monsters."

"Yeah, some of the details of the dreams I have are fuzzy. But so far, no big monsters."

Anne smiled. "Dreams can also help us understand the difficult challenges we worry about, like getting that letter to your father. Your grandmother believes that we often see the future in our dreams and that if we're lucky, we can bring special gifts back from our dreams into waking life. So maybe you really held that four-leaf clover in your imagination for a short time. Perhaps the biggest gift from your dream will be the story you'll write and illustrate."

"Mom, do you think Riverwood Hollow in my dream might

really be like Grandma's place? Can I see it when we are there for Christmas?"

"If the weather isn't too cold, we'll take a walk together. It sounds like your dream took place in the summertime. We'll have to wait for summer to explore the area when there are dragonflies and four-leaf clovers. You can spend time with your grandma over summer vacation."

"And maybe I'll find another four-leaf clover."

Anne laughed. "That's right. I know how much you like playing games on your electronic tablet. But how about keeping a journal where you can write about your adventures and draw some pictures? It'll make a great story to tell. Everyone likes an interesting story. Maybe you could draw a map of your dream world like the one you found in the magic mailbox."

"That's a great idea!" Travis exclaimed.

"Since we are stuck here tonight and maybe even tomorrow, I'd like to give a courageous and brave, young boy an early gift."

Anne pulled a red leather journal from her tote bag and slid it across the table. "You already have pencils, but I also bought a Harry Potter pen. It's a magic pen. It will help you record the magic you experience in your dreams."

"Mom, thank you so much! I'm really glad you believed me about my dreams. I thought you might say they were silly or made-up, stupid stuff."

"Travis, I would never say that. I know some adults say, 'It's only a dream,' when a child talks about a dream, especially a scary one. It sounds like you've had a glorious adventure. And I can't wait to hear more. Some native people believe that there's a place called the dreamtime, and it is as real as the life we live every day."

"I knew my dream had to be real," Travis said, and Squirrel felt the squeeze of the boy's hand.

Having lost interest in the bowl of nuts, Squirrel had listened carefully to the conversation between Travis and his mother. He had lots of questions about the dream Travis described. Where had the four-leaf clover gone? Why was he separated from Travis in Riverwood Hollow? Would the letter be delivered to Travis's father? Was it possible his experiences in Riverwood Hollow, like those of Travis, were all just part of a crazy dream and didn't mean a thing? Or did they happen in a real place?

Squirrel was curious about what Travis might draw and write about. He wondered if Travis would figure out that they each were visiting the same place in the dream world. It was obvious to Squirrel that they both had met the same lady wearing purple running shoes.

Then he remembered Anne's words, for they seemed very important. "Where there's love, there's magic, even miracles, especially at Christmastime."

Chapter 13

The Point at the Great Turning

Let the wild rumpus start!

—Maurice Sendak, *Where the Wild Things Are*

Squirrel scanned the hotel's expansive atrium as Travis and his mother rode the glass elevator up to their room on the top floor. The elevator itself resembled a giant tree, like the ones he climbed in his dreams. The hotel's vaulted ceiling, which sheltered a dozen floors circling the lobby and restaurant, reminded him of the sky overlooking the forest of Riverwood Hollow. Birds flew around inside the hotel's open spaces. Squirrel wondered if they had been trapped there by mistake, maybe like being stuck inside a dream. Peering through the glass wall of the ascending elevator, he remembered climbing the tree where he had met Baldwin.

While Anne unpacked some of her belongings, Travis placed Squirrel on the windowsill. Their room had a window view of the area surrounding the airport. His position enabled him to survey the grounds around the hotel entrance and also see the inside of the hotel room.

"Look at all the snow. This is so cool," Travis said, petting his head.

Squirrel looked down at the thick layer of white stuff that buried the walkways and parking lot. He wondered what snow felt like and if Baldwin had ever been in a snowstorm in Riverwood Hollow. When he heard Anne speak to Travis, Squirrel turned his attention from the snow to hear the conversation behind his back.

"We've got two queen beds. Travis, you and the squirrel can have the bed next to the window. Staying in this hotel is a luxury I can appreciate after our travel difficulties. I've got a feeling we may be here longer than one night. I'll check with the airlines in the morning and see if there's a flight without having to fly standby. If not, I'll book us for a departure on the following day. We'll still arrive in time for your grandmother's Christmas Eve dinner."

"Mom, this place is awesome. Did you see all the balcony walkways and rooms overlooking the restaurant on the ground floor?"

Anne nodded and pointed to a small refrigerator. "We're also well supplied with drinks and a cabinet full of snacks too. We'll be fine if the storm continues."

Travis put squirrel on top of one of the bed pillows. "And there are two elevators. It's like we're living in a nest at the top of a couple huge trees. Squirrel and I will have fun exploring the hotel." Squirrel smiled, hearing that Travis thought the elevators were like trees too.

"It's been a long day, so I won't turn on the TV," Anne said. "I'll call your dad and grandmother tomorrow. I'll let them know about our arrangements after I find out about our next flights. I messaged them both while you were in the bathroom at the airport. They've been worried about us."

"Is dad OK? Did you tell him about my letter?"

"He's fine, still working late. I didn't mention the letter but told him that you missed him terribly. I understand how hard it is for you to be without him this Christmas, and I know he feels bad about not being with us. He said to tell you he loves you. For now, let's get some sleep. Sweet dreams, dear Travis. I love you."

"I love you too, Mom."

Squirrel closed his eyes hearing the word *love* and welcomed the tingling warmth that spread through his chest as Travis hugged him. But he worried about Travis and how sad he felt, missing his father. At least they were safe from the storm and the problems at the airport. Nothing could go wrong now.

*

Squirrel found himself in a pile of mulch beneath a bird feeder. Brushing wet twigs from his fur, he scratched his head and climbed to the top of a boulder where he could get a view of his surroundings. He hoped to find Baldwin but saw only a small cottage that faced the path along the river. "It's c ... cold," he chittered. "Where's the sun?"

"Hey, Squirrel, where have you been?"

Squirrel jumped to the ground and circled around toward the sound of his princely friend's raspy voice. "Baldwin, I was just thinking about you."

"Winter weather is on its way," Baldwin said.

"I've been with my boy in a warmer place," Squirrel replied.

"Boy? Oh yeah. Remember when your friend the hawk was talking about that boy mailing a letter to his dad at the magic mailbox? I forgot to tell you. I also saw him with a letter in his hand, standing next to that mailbox. Did you know there's a blue heron living on the pond right behind the mailbox?"

Squirrel flicked his tail several times, feeling irritated by Baldwin's shift in the conversation. "This place is so confusing. I don't care about a blue heron. But I remember that pond. I wonder if I can find Travis there."

"We can look for the boy later. Let's get some nuts," Baldwin said. "The crone who was helping the boy lives in this cottage. She puts out squirrel food in the bowl beneath the bird feeders. Maybe your boy is with her."

Squirrel approached the bowl sitting on the patio and sniffed. Then he backed up and ran around the bowl, not sure what to do next. Seeing Baldwin nibbling a nut, he scampered to the bowl a second time. He grabbed one nut and raced to the magnolia tree that was growing near the feeders. Climbing onto a branch, he almost dropped the nut. He eventually figured out how to sit up and balance on the slim branch with his back legs while holding the nut in his front two paws.

Baldwin laughed. "Squirrel, you must get tougher if you're going to survive winter weather."

"I've never experienced winter outside before," Squirrel said. He thought about how the big squirrel had saved him from certain death in another dream. Now he wondered if he could possibly die in this world and never return to his life as a squirrel puppet in the boy's world.

Baldwin scratched his ears. "Yeah, winter's a big shock with the ice, snow, and freezing temperatures. I remember my first winter.

The spongy forest floor on the banks of the river froze to a sheet of slippery ice. The misty meadows quilted with wildflowers became frosted fields of dried grass, fenced by leafless trees. Our lively emerald forest turned silent. Its magic went into hiding. I guess I'm getting too poetic."

"How do you know all those fancy ways of talking?" Squirrel asked.

"The woman who supplies these tasty nuts likes to quote poetry. I listen to her when she sits on the porch behind her cottage."

Squirrel smiled and tilted his head. "Just like you, I used to listen to humans who visited the gift shop where I lived as a puppet in my other life. That's how I learned words for things."

"You told me that others in your world called you Squirrel. How come you don't have a real name?"

Squirrel hesitated, not knowing how to answer the question or what to tell Baldwin first. "I don't have a name that I know of. In the gift shop, all the puppet animals had tags attached to their paws. Each tag had a name. I had a tag but no name. So my friends called me Squirrel. When the boy Travis bought me, he tore the tag off and took me away from the shop. I left all my friends on the puppet tree. Now I live with the boy as his playmate. He calls me Squirrel too."

Baldwin grimaced. "I recall something about a name tag in my past life too. Every creature deserves a name. Tell me more about your other life."

"Well, when I am not here, I live in that other world," Squirrel said. "Things aren't the same. I can't move around like I do here. The animals who are my friends were left back at the gift shop. They're all different, like Wings the hawk. You've met him. I also saw some of them once in a dream here in Riverwood Hollow too."

Baldwin grinned. "I remember a place in another world where I once lived. It was a long time ago, and the memories have faded. I was stuck in the corner of a window display, and I never got moved. I was there so long I got bored and decided to stay in this world instead. Maybe I was in a gift shop too. I hope you find a name like I found a life."

Squirrel sighed. "I've heard stories about squirrels who were famous. I've always wanted a name that would make me famous. But now I just want to be with my friends, and my name is not as important. I'm getting used to being called Squirrel. I even like it."

Baldwin stood up on his hind legs and sniffed the air. "Hey, I know a special place I'd like to show you, before we get too much snow. We can go to the mailbox and the pond on the way and look for your boy."

Suddenly, snow began to fall, and the wind picked up. Within a few minutes, the flurries grew thicker, quickly covering the trees and ground with a blanket of white flakes. Squirrel shivered, shaking ice crystals from his inflated tail. "The snow is sticking to my fur!"

"You're a strange little squirrel," Baldwin said.

"But no stranger than this world!" said a voice he'd heard before in his dreams.

Squirrel wiped snow from his face and looked up. The hawk perched on a branch over their heads. "Wings! You're back."

"Listen to me, silly squirrels," the hawk said. "I just saw a big storm coming. You've got to take cover."

"Nah, it's just a few flakes," Baldwin said. "I'm going to take Squirrel to the Point."

"The point of what?" Wings asked, nodding his beak in the direction of Baldwin's chest.

Baldwin waved his frosted tail back and forth. "Don't you know anything about this place with all your flying? The Point is where the river turns. We call it the Point at the Great Turning. Squirrel will love exploring beyond the pond and that mailbox. The storm won't hit for a while."

"Looking at you Baldwin, all I know is I'm suddenly very hungry," Wings said, spreading his wings.

Squirrel watched Wings lift off the branch where he had been perched, relieved the hawk didn't view Baldwin as his next meal. Then he realized how distracted he'd been by Baldwin's chatter and the nuts in the crone's dish. Would he ever find Travis in this dream place?

Chapter 14

The Fork in the Road

Never Give up ... No one knows
what's going to happen next.

—L. Frank Baum, *The Patchwork Girl of Oz*

Travis entered the path that snaked through the tunnel of twined trees. This time, it was coated with a layer of snow. As he emerged onto the gravel road, he noticed flames rising from a fire ring in the familiar field near the magic mailbox. A lone figure stood over the fire, poking it with a long stick. As he approached the figure, he saw the purple shoes.

"Ah, there you are, my boy," the old woman said.

Raising his eyes to hers, Travis said, "I still don't know your name, but you know mine."

The woman's eyes glinted in the light of the flames, and her mouth turned upward in a smile. "I've known you all your life, and names don't matter right now."

"I must be in a dream again," he said. "What's happening in this dream?"

"You can't always predict what will happen in a dream, just like waking life, I might add."

Travis scrunched his forehead, trying to make sense of what the woman was saying. "I'm confused."

"Let's go to the end of the gravel road," the woman said, leading Travis across the snowy field. "Just a few more steps, and you'll see something that marks the intersection between two footpaths."

Travis pulled his jacket up around his neck and surveyed the area. He wondered what he was supposed to be seeing other than the snow-covered magic mailbox.

The old woman pointed to a short tree stump surrounded by green grass and flowering vines. "There! There it is! Do you see the fork stuck in the tree stump? It's a fork in the road."

Travis blinked. The fork embedded in the top of the stump was the strangest thing he'd ever seen. The fork itself was an ordinary utensil like one he'd used for eating a meal. The entire post looked out of place, as though it was still the middle of summer in that single spot. The rest of the area was covered in ice and snow.

"I see it," Travis said. "Why would a person put a fork in a tree stump? It's just a regular fork like I eat with. And why are there leaves and vines around it? It's winter. There should be snow there."

"It's not an ordinary place," the woman replied. "It marks a moment when a person needs to make a choice."

"But this is a dream. How can a choice made in this place matter in real life?"

The woman's eyes narrowed. "Some events spill from one world into the next. A choice made in your dream can affect the other world, the one you call the real world."

"Do I need to make a choice about something?" Travis asked.

"Sometimes the choice to be made belongs to someone else. Here, let me show you what I mean. Look closely at the fork."

Travis stepped into the green grass that surrounded the tree stump. He stared at the fork. Unexpectedly, the fork disappeared. Where the fork had been stuck in the stump an image appeared.

"It's my father!" Travis exclaimed. Then, rubbing his chest, he looked more closely at the image.

"Yes, your father, Thomas," the woman affirmed.

Thomas was sitting at a desk piled with folders, reading. As Travis continued to stare at the flickering scene, tears formed in his eyes. He wanted to call out to him, but the words stuck in his throat.

When his father stood up and pushed aside his chair, Travis

noticed a picture of his mother holding him when he was a baby sitting on his father's desk. He also saw his most recent school picture and another one of the three of them when they had a picnic last summer in a park outside Duval, Washington. Travis tried to hold on to the image of that picture, but gradually it faded, and the fork shimmered in its place.

"A boy must keep dreaming and expect things to work out," the woman said.

Travis pulled his backpack off his shoulder and opened the top compartment, searching for Squirrel. "The squirrel's still not here, and I've lost the map too. I need directions to find him."

"You'll most likely find your friend again. No need to look for the map right now. Besides, the most important part of the map was its message."

"It was about courage," Travis said, lifting the backpack to his shoulder.

"Courage asks each of us to make choices in different ways," the old woman added as she vanished into the shimmering fork.

Chapter 15

Stranded

We are going nowhere.
That my friend, is the irony of our constant movement.

—Rebecca Rupp, *The Dragon of Lonely Island*

Travis awoke the next morning while his mother was on the phone. Keeping his eyes closed, he pulled the sheet over his head and pretended to be asleep. Then he remembered the dream about the fork in the road and his father's image. He wondered if his father had received his letter. And who was the woman who wore purple running shoes and talked about choice and consequences? She said she'd known him all of his life. Maybe she was his grandmother. Hearing his mother sigh, he peeked over the top of the sheet.

"Yes, I understand," Anne said, pacing in front of the bathroom door. "First class would be perfect. Book us on that early-morning flight for tomorrow. It'll be easier than flying standby all day with a child."

When Anne ended the call, Travis sat up in bed. "Mom, are we going to be here for another night?"

"Yes. I am so sorry about another delay. But we can use the day to read and watch TV. I'll call your father and grandmother later this morning. I have some playing cards in my carry-on. I used to play solitaire with my grandmother. It's really fun."

Travis jumped out of bed. "Mom, if you don't mind, I'll leave card playing and TV watching to you. Squirrel and I have plans to explore the hotel. We'll go on an adventure, riding up and down the glass elevators to all the floors. I'll take my journal with me so I can make up stories."

"Just be careful, and don't talk to strangers. And don't leave the hotel. I'll sit in the lobby to keep an eye on you. I don't want you to go out of my sight."

"Oh, Mom!"

"And while you're exploring, you might draw some of your adventures. When you imagine a story, it's a lot like dreaming."

Travis opened his backpack and pulled out a package of colored pencils. "I just had a really good idea. I'll make a map of this hotel like Riverwood Hollow in my dream. The stories will be like my dreams. The elevators still remind me of huge trees."

"That's a great idea. You mentioned that before when we rode up to our room yesterday. Maybe you can think of the world tree in the Norse myth. You remember, where the squirrel Ratatoskr races up and down that tree between the eagle perched at the top and the dragon sitting at the bottom. With your squirrel, you could imagine new stories."

"Mom, you've told me about Ratatoskr lots of times. Ratatoskr passes messages between everyone on the tree, spreading rumors and gossip."

Anne laughed. "Well, I hope your squirrel understands the importance of passing messages of love rather than ones of confusion and mistrust. The world has enough of those right now."

"I know, Mom. I've seen the news on TV. My squirrel's going to be a superhero."

"Perhaps like that raccoon hero in the movies you like so much," Anne added.

*

Travis spent most of the day wandering around the balconies that overlooked the lobby and restaurant. Clutching Squirrel under his arm, he rode the two elevators up and down. He imagined them as one great world tree with an up ladder and a down ladder.

Each area of the hotel he pictured as part of Riverwood Hollow. The boxes stacked in the storage area behind the elevators on the first floor became a dense forest that was impossible to penetrate. The ice machines on the balconies served as weather clouds that produced snow. The whirlpool in the fitness center, when turned on, swirled like the dangerous part of a river. The bronze-colored mailbox in the lobby he named the magic mailbox. He even discovered a fork on a log next to an indoor fireplace. Every time he thought he was alone, he noticed his mother lurking around the corner, watching his every move.

For lunch, he ate pizza and root beer while he illustrated his dreamlike story. He charged his meal to the room number registered in his mother's name. The server didn't question the charge. She was the same one who helped them at dinner when they first arrived at the hotel. By the late afternoon, he become tired and decided to return to the room and see what might be on TV.

His mother met him at the door to their room. She pressed the card key against the electronic sensor on the door and pushed it open. The beds were made, the curtains were open, and two fresh bottles of water sat on the desk. Travis set his journal on the nightstand and exhaled in satisfaction over the story and illustrations he had created as Anne closed the curtains and turned on the TV.

Pulling Squirrel to his face, Travis laid his head on the down pillow and turned on the light next to his bed. He had intended to watch the film about winter in Yellowstone National Park on the National Geographic channel. But instead, he drifted to sleep, thinking about the letter to his father.

Chapter 16

Dreaming Together

I think we dream so we don't have
to be apart for so long.
If we're in each other's dreams, we
can be together all the time.

—A. A. Milne, *Winnie-the-Pooh*

Travis emerged from the same tunnel passage he had traveled through during his previous dream. This time, the field was buried beneath a layer of snow. Only the top of the magic mailbox and its red flag could be seen above a snowdrift that had blown over the intersection at the end of the gravel road. A row of trees loomed overhead like frozen ghosts, and the sky shone a dazzling blue beneath a bright sun.

Relieved to be dressed in a winter jacket, Travis scanned the area and traipsed through the snow to the magic mailbox. He pulled the backpack off his shoulder, kicked aside the snow, and set it on the ground. Suspecting his puppet would be missing, he unzipped the pockets and searched all the compartments. He found the frog, tablet, bendable action figure, his journal, pencils, bag of tiny superheroes, and an extra cookie from the airplane. "Squirrel's gone again?" he cried, stuffing his belongings back into the backpack.

"I do believe that Squirrel may be wondering where you are."

Travis looked up in surprise. A hawk sat on top of the mailbox. "Did you just say something?" he asked.

"Of course. Everyone can talk," the hawk replied. "OK, you guys, you can come out now."

Travis stood in silence, not knowing how to respond as a group of animals emerged from the snowy trees. An orange cat with mangy fur around his face led the way. Following the cat came a raccoon with a white heart on its stomach and an opossum with a pink nose and long white tail. A painted turtle brought up the rear, plodding several feet behind the others. His face barely extended beyond the edge of its shell. A dragon flew above them all, exhaling a stream of smoke as it shapeshifted into a variety of colors and sizes.

Travis tried to move toward the animals, but his feet were frozen to the ground. Still bewildered, he managed to utter a few words. "Hey, you're like the puppets in the gift shop!"

"Yes indeed," the hawk said. "I saw you mail a letter to your father. Being Squirrel's best friend, I've been concerned about how unhappy you've been. Therefore, I gathered up Squirrel's puppet friends from our tree of life and—"

"You are the animals from the gift shop," Travis declared. "I remember the names on your tags. You're Wings. And the cat is Roar, the raccoon is Bandita, the opossum is Pinkie, and that turtle, Shell something or other."

"Shelltin's the name," the turtle asserted, sticking his head out farther from his protective shell.

"But I never saw a dragon on the puppet tree," Travis said, staring at the dragon that had landed on the mailbox next to Wings.

"My name's Fire," said the dragon. "I was dumped in the return box behind the cash register before you came in the gift shop. But I caught a glimpse of you with Squirrel when you left with your mom."

"Glad to meet you, Fire, but how did all of you get here? I mean ..."

"Friends want to be together, and we missed Squirrel," replied Wings. "It's easier than you think to share a dream when everyone's part of the same tribe. We decided to dream our way here. Fire taught us how ... after he got out of the return box. Now it's time to hatch a plan to find Squirrel before the next storm moves through. The weather changes rapidly in this place."

"Where is Squirrel?" Travis demanded.

"He got chased by a dog and is hanging out with another obnoxious squirrel named Baldwin."

"He has a new friend?" Travis asked.

"Baldwin's telling Squirrel he is a princely friend, whatever that means," Wings added, narrowing his eyes.

"How can we find him?" Travis wondered. "I had a map, but I don't have it anymore."

Roar padded up next to Travis. "Boy, what good is a map if you can't find it or if you don't even know where to look for what needs to be found?"

Bandita crept up next to Roar and stood up on her hind legs. "That's the thing about this place. It's tricky. You never know what's going to happen next. But there's a way to find what you love ... if you're dreaming with a big heart."

Pinkie nudged the babies that clung to her back and waddled around Roar and Bandita. "Talk about tricky. I even had to play dead once when a crazed dog named Brutus raced through the trees. And I don't understand where all these babies came from. They kept showing up. Now I have to protect them and carry them around on my back."

"And I can't make anyone listen to me!" exclaimed Roar with a high-pitched meow.

Without warning, Fire swooped down in front of the cat and

tossed his head in the air. A sizzling ball of fire erupted from his mouth. "Roar, you can't roar anymore, and you're too small to protect us. Wings is in charge."

Roar hissed. "Listen, you overgrown lizard, it's getting really cold. I bet you won't like it when more snow falls and you've shapeshifted into a dragonfly."

The hawk flapped his wings and glared at everyone until each one fell silent. "We're Squirrel's friends. We won't solve our problems with all this backbiting. The boy wants to find Squirrel. But more importantly, if any of you had any vision at all, you'd see what's obvious. I heard about the letter the boy mailed to his father at that so-called magic mailbox, and I figured it all out. He wants his father to come home for Christmas. The boy wants to be with his family, and Squirrel needs to be with his family too."

Travis held up his hands. "That's enough! Yes, I want to find Squirrel. And I hope the letter will reach my father and he'll decide to come to Grandma's for Christmas. But how do you guys think you can help?"

"Well, I just happen to know Squirrel's probable location," Wings said as he raised his right talon and pointed toward the path on the right side of the pond. "He's exploring. Just before a big snowstorm, Baldwin led him down that path to the end of the hollow where the river makes a turn. We have to go beyond the maze of trails where turtles dig nests in warmer weather. The trail through the woods is buried beneath snow and twists through ice-covered bushes. I should have eaten that fat squirrel, Baldwin, days ago."

Travis wanted to say something to defend Squirrel's new friend. Squeezing out the words, he managed a whisper. "No, you can't do that."

Wings dipped his wing toward Travis. "I guess I'm frustrated with the situation. I'll fly overhead and keep an eye on you guys ... as soon as I find something else to eat."

After Wings lifted off the branch, Roar pushed into the center of the other animals. "I know about courage. And this boy has it. I'm sure we can rescue Squirrel from that trickster squirrel if the boy helps us."

Scanning the trail, Travis pulled a hood from his jacket over his head. "It's now or never. We must have courage," he said. Worrying about Squirrel being buried in a snowdrift, he picked up the turtle and then his backpack before stepping into the woods. Trekking forward, he became concerned about the animals behind him, so he paused and looked back. In a single-file line, Roar padded behind him, and Bandita scurried behind the cat. Pinkie waddled after the raccoon while mumbling about keeping her babies safe as Fire flew overhead. Travis's feet broke through the ice-crusted trail as he led the way.

Moments later, the wind gusted. Clouds raced across the sun, releasing a deluge of snow, concealing the path ahead. Travis stopped and looked up, wishing the hawk would return. But he saw only more falling snow. "How can the weather change so quickly?" he said, turning toward the animals behind him. "It was sunny just a while ago."

"We've got to keep going," Roar said, glancing up at the tops of the trees. "I'm sure we'll find a safe place to hide from the storm. Don't worry. There's a lion watching over everyone. He says we'll find our way. There's a cave beneath the roots of a tree I remember seeing in a vision. It's just ahead."

"It's a blizzard!" screamed Pinkie. "My babies are covered in snow."

Travis stopped to brush the snow from Pinkie's fur and wipe it from the tiny opossums' faces. Then he patted her on the head. "It's going to be OK," he said. During times like this, he missed his father more than ever. It was hard being an only child with only animals as friends, and now to make matters worse, he was responsible for their well-being.

Then he remembered words from another dream. Feeling braver, he whispered to himself, "Adventures are for courageous souls. It's a quality one has when doing something for love. I only wish I had that map and my father."

Chapter 17

The Great River Tree

Don't you know everyone's got a Fairyland of their own?

—P. L. Travers, *Mary Poppins*

Squirrel leaned against the massive trunk of a towering tree anchored on the riverbank. Peering through wafting snow flurries, he noticed an alarming amount of trash washed up onto the banks of the river. Plastic bottles and soda cans lay scattered among exposed roots and patches of ice lining the shoreline.

"Baldwin, where are you?" Squirrel whispered, closing his eyes and nodding off.

"Squirrel, wake up!"

Squirrel opened his eyes and glanced up. Wings was barely visible, perched on an ice-covered branch midway up the tree.

"Wings, I don't want to wake up. I'm dreaming," Squirrel yelled, before scaling up to a branch below Wings.

"Waking up is not about getting out of a dream. It's about staying awake inside the dream, so you end up where you want to be," Wings said.

"You sound like Roar when he talks with smart words."

"He's not smart enough to escape his nightmare living as a domestic cat," Wings said. "He stalks mice and chipmunks under fallen logs, eats bugs, and meows like a kitten."

"Poor Roar," Squirrel said. He felt sorry for the lion but thought he might have a lesson to learn in humility.

Wings fluffed his tail feathers. "And there's something really weird about Roar. I've caught him talking to himself more than once. He thinks he's having a conversation with a great lion spirit living among the branches of the tallest trees. The lion's been giving him advice. Sometimes Roar's clueless about the seasons and acts like he's in another time and place."

Squirrel scratched his ears, looking at the path he and Baldwin had traveled. His tail stiffened as he watched snow blow over his paw prints, completely covering them. "I'm freezing," he said, shivering. "Roar never believed in dreaming when we were in the gift shop. But he is still king of our puppet tree, and I don't want to think about his lion spirit in the treetops right now."

"I guess he's learning about dreams though," Wings said.

"And maybe something about himself," Squirrel added. "Can we talk about something other than Roar? Like how to get out of this weather!"

In the next moment, Baldwin scampered up the tree into the niche where Squirrel sat. "Don't count on good weather anymore for a while. One day a few months from now, this sycamore tree will have branches so thick with leaves you can hide from a certain winged predator who might be hunting his next meal."

Wings laughed. "I can see through leafy branches, especially when certain animals flick bushy tails."

Squirrel remained silent, considering Baldwin's words. Was it possible Wings was developing new appetites in Riverwood Hollow, like squirrel meat?

Squirrel climbed farther up the trunk away from Baldwin so he could face Wings eye to eye. Horrified by what he saw, he stopped short of the hawk's talons and placed a paw on his throat. Fresh blood dripped from the branch where Wings stood on top of a clump of gray fur.

"Wings, what have you done?" Squirrel gasped, pointing to the traces of crimson liquid on the blotched bark.

"Just an injured baby rabbit," Wings replied, his eyes gleaming.

"We all need to eat. I don't like nuts, seeds, and acorns. That's right. I see it on your face. You're wondering if I would dine on your furry flesh. I think not. Your tail is not too appealing; not much meat, too much fur. Plus, a hawk like me doesn't eat his friends, at least not that I can foresee in the future."

Squirrel didn't think it was possible for a hawk to smile. Yet a smirk spread across Wing's face, and his eyes turned a blazing red. Squirrel cringed, recalling those eyes on previous occasions. He pawed his chest where his heart thumped louder than he wished. "I'll remember your promise not to eat friends," he said with a quivering voice.

"And one whose name you know," Baldwin added, joining Squirrel and Wings on the same branch.

"Humor aside," Wings said, "do you know what kind of tree you're sitting in, other than my tree?"

"I just woke up. Remember?" Squirrel barked. He still felt doubtful about the hawk's possible intentions about not eating a squirrel.

Wings folded his wings around his fluffy white chest feathers, looking as though he were dressed in a fine winter cloak. "This is the tallest tree on the river, a sycamore, as you guys already know.

Notice how enormous it is. Its branches reach into the sky and touch the clouds. You're sitting in the Great River Tree, the most important tree in the area, right here at the Point. I'm the bird who'll be nesting at the top, keeping an eye on the comings and goings in the hollow."

"Wings is correct. This is where the White River turns," Baldwin said.

Squirrel peered up at the tree's twisting boughs forming a wide umbrella over the river. "I never know what to expect in a dream."

Wings nodded. "Perhaps you'll remember another friend. Fire naps inside a cave beneath the roots of this snow-covered tree. He's a shapeshifter now. In warmer weather, he hovers over the weeds along the river as a dragonfly. During colder days, he appears as a scaly lizard who warms his lair with his breath."

"Fire the dragon? But I thought he was with that little girl and her sister who purchased him in the gift shop."

"I tried to tell you about Fire before when we were talking about dragonflies. But Baldwin kept interrupting, and then you disappeared. Fire was bought. But the girls changed their minds. He was left in the store's return box on top of a pile of other rejected purchases. Later he told us that the dream world is a place where we all can meet, no matter where we're living."

Unexpectedly, Fire stuck his head out from the back side of the trunk and crawled onto the branch where Wings and the two squirrels sat. Puffing a bit of smoke into the air, he slapped Squirrel on the back with his long claws. "Great to see you, my confused friend." Then turning to Wings, he added, "They're coming down the path."

"A dragon! I've seen too much today. See you guys later," Baldwin chittered, descending the tree trunk. His tail waved in circles as he raced to the trunk of a nearby pine tree.

"Fire, it's really you! I am so glad to see you!" exclaimed Squirrel. "I thought you'd been lost to the pink princesses. But you don't look the same, not as fierce looking as I remember, and a little smaller too."

Fire raised his head toward the sky and puffed a longer stream of smoke. "I try to avoid burning down the forest with my flaming voice. About my size, we all have different experiences in the dream world. Unlike Roar, I can adapt to the situation with my shapeshifting. Dragons have that kind of magic. In this place, most of the time, I'm the dragon guardian of the Great River Tree, and I stay close to its roots."

Squirrel scratched his head and flicked snow from his tail. "Fire, my dreams are so hard to understand. Every time I dream, the place is different. The weather and the scenery change. That's confusing enough. Shapeshifting is almost unbelievable."

"Most disconcerting," Fire agreed. "Time here is fluid. Sometimes you might even drop into future time so that you learn something before it happens. That's how I knew so much about this place back when we talked in the gift shop. This Great River Tree is bit like our puppet tree, a world tree."

"I know about Squirrel Ratatoskr and the world tree in old myths," Squirrel said as a blizzard of falling snow blurred his vision. "He caused lots of trouble. I don't want to be that kind of squirrel."

The hawk flapped his wings. "Squirrel, listen to me. I've heard about that story too. To begin with, I'm the bird at the top of this tree, not an eagle. This hawk has vision second to no other bird. The dragon at the bottom of our tree tells all kinds of stories about dreaming. Sometimes I wish he'd go back to napping and keep his theories about this place to himself. I prefer flying and eating to talking."

"Then stop talking!" Fire scolded, nodding his head at the ground below. "The storm is getting worse, and I can barely see our friends. Look down!"

Squirrel couldn't believe his eyes. "It's my boy! And Roar!"

Travis stopped and looked up. "Squirrel?"

*

Travis woke up and noticed that Squirrel was no longer in the bed. He swept his hands through the sheets and the comforter, searching for him. Then he slid out of bed and pushed aside the curtain to the window. It was dark outside. The lights at the hotel entrance illuminated the snow-covered streets. A blue truck with a snow blade moved back and forth through the parking lot. Piles of snow dotted the area.

"Have I slept through the night?" Travis said as he shuffled toward the bathroom. Just before climbing back into bed, he discovered Squirrel on the floor. Picking him up, he brushed his hand through his fur. Squirrel was cold, and his feet were wet. "When I couldn't find you in the bed, I thought I'd lost you. But just like in my dream, I found you."

Chapter 18

Snowbound

It is when we are most lost that we
find our truest friends.

—Brothers Grimm, *Snow White*

"Travis, you were talking in your sleep," Anne said. "Did you have a good nap?"

"I was dreaming about Squirrel. I lost him. When I woke up, I found him on the floor. What time is it? It's dark outside."

"It's seven o'clock. We need to get some dinner. Let's go down to the restaurant and then stop at the gift shop. When I called the airlines, I was told the storm is moving on and that they are clearing the runways. It looks like we'll make our flight in the morning."

Later that evening, Travis helped his mother pack their bags before setting the alarm for an early-morning checkout. As he prepared for bed, he held Squirrel up to his face. "Stay close. I don't want to lose you again."

*

Squirrel landed in a pile of snow. Shaking his fur, he lifted his head and peered at the frost-covered trees that lined the icy path. The hollow was buried beneath what looked like the puffy comforter from the bed in the hotel room. Where were Travis and his friends? He had seen them in his last dream. Now they had disappeared.

The Great River Tree loomed ahead of him, spreading its branches over water that no longer flowed. He tried running toward the trunk of the sycamore but sunk so deep into the snow that only his head remained uncovered.

"Squirrel, is that you? It's me, Roar!"

"Roar, I hear you, but I can't see you. Where am I?"

"You're caught in a massive snowdrift. A rather deplorable situation, I might add."

Squirrel found a foothold on a large rock and pushed himself up to the snow's surface. When he wiped the moisture from his face, he saw Roar peering down at him from the top of a fallen log.

"It's so cold my tail's frozen stiff," Squirrel chittered as his eyes met Roar's. The cat's big gold eyes were the same that belonged to the lion he'd known in the gift shop.

"It's a blizzard," Roar bellowed. "We must go to our shelter in the roots of the Great River Tree. Follow me now!" Squirrel ran after Roar as he crossed the frozen ground toward the base of the tree's trunk. "Quick! We must get inside out of the weather."

"But where are the others?" Squirrel asked. "I thought everyone was here. I saw the boy and all the puppets in another dream."

"Stop asking questions," Roar hissed. "Everyone is here, in the cave beneath the tree." Roar began digging up frozen leaves around its roots.

Squirrel felt sorry for the cat, watching him exert so much effort to dig a hole in the snow. He could only imagine Roar's frustration at not being his normal lion self.

A few moments later, Roar pointed to a hole in the roots just wide enough for each of them to squeeze through one at a time. "Here's the entrance," he said.

Squirrel shivered and shook his head. "Do I really have to go into that hole?"

"Trust me, Squirrel. I'll go first."

Once beyond the entrance, Squirrel found himself in a gloomy space where it was nearly impossible for him to see anything. He squinted, brushing the snow and dirt from his eyes. "Where is everyone? It's dark in here."

"I know, but we're safe from the snowstorm," Roar said. "I'll push away some of the snow covering the hole above us. That might help until it gets dark."

Roar scratched at a space above the roots, and a thin stream of light fell through the opening. It was enough for Squirrel to get a better look at the cat. He couldn't help staring at what had become of the old lion he once knew. Roar's small mane was matted with tangled bits and pieces of twigs, leaves, and bristly weeds. He looked like an ordinary cat left to fend for himself.

Roar's familiar grin shone through his dirty face. "I know, it's a shock to see me like this. But perhaps you'll recognize the rest of our tree-of-life tribe."

Squirrel scanned the cave. Shelltin sat unmoving in a corner next to a pile of small branches. Fire lounged in the midst of a cloud of smoke, tending a tiny fire contained by a ring of stones. Bandita and Pinkie huddled together next to Travis. Three baby opossums clung to Pinkie's back.

Travis leaped to his feet, bumping his head against a dripping root. "Squirrel! It's you!" he called. "I thought I found you, but then you disappeared. I'm so glad you're safe."

"Finally, I'm out of the snow," Squirrel replied, moving toward the boy.

Travis knelt down and began scraping away a compost of leaves from the ground near an outcropping of the tree's roots. "Here, Squirrel. I've cleared a space for us."

"No!" screamed Pinkie. "A snake!"

Before Squirrel reached Travis, the opossum intercepted his path. She scrambled to Travis and ducked her head into a hole in the roots. Without hesitation, she grabbed a long black snake in her mouth and carried it toward the opening to the cave. The snake thrashed against the side of her face, and the babies squirmed around her back as she wiggled through the snowy entrance.

Travis crawled to where Squirrel sat. He picked him up and drew him close. "I'm scared, and I wish my father were here. He could help us."

Squirrel held his paws against his rapidly beating heart and gasped in relief. He pushed his head against Travis's jacket, hoping there weren't any other snakes in their hiding place. Other than one of the snake puppets hanging on the gift shop tree, he had never seen a snake. He wondered how he and the other puppets could help Travis be with his father. "I know how much you love him," he whispered, peering up at Travis. "I'm scared too."

A tear dropped down the boy's face. "I just want my mom and dad to be together and for all of us to be a family again. It's Christmas. And I don't like snakes!"

"It's a good thing Pinkie saw that snake," Fire said, puffing out a ring of smoke.

"And it's a good thing Fire dug out this cave before we were all buried in snow," Shelltin said. "Now he keeps us warm."

Pinkie returned to the cave, dragging her frozen tail as she waddled around a curtain of mossy cobwebs. She adjusted the babies clinging to her back and crawled toward the fire.

Fire pulled her into a firm embrace. "You're a brave mother. You saved the boy's life. Let me warm you with my toasty scales."

"It wasn't venomous," she said. "Just an ordinary black rat snake. I happened to see its head before it dropped back into the hole in the roots. I dropped it into another tree root downstream."

After the excitement died down about the snake, Squirrel looked around the cave, checking on his friends. "Where's Wings?"

Bandita twitched her whiskers as she plodded toward him from the far corner of the cave. Her eyes were now visible from within her mask of dark fur. "He's got a nest in a hole at the top of the tree where he stands guard for us. And there's this dumb squirrel named Baldwin who runs up and down the tree, delivering messages. He's good with the snow and wants to talk to everyone all the time. For the life of me, I can never understand anything he's talking about."

Squirrel wasn't surprised by Baldwin's behavior. He hoped the big squirrel didn't distract his friends from more important matters … like food. "Is there anything to eat around here?" he asked.

"We're in luck," Pinkie said. "That crazy lady with the purple shoes puts out all kinds of delicious stuff on her patio and lots of seeds in the bird feeders.

Roar slumped down onto his front paws. "Squirrel, I didn't believe you when you talked about this dream world. I'm a believer now. Plus, I know what it's like to be an ordinary cat. I eat mice, bugs, and dry cat food, if I'm lucky. Maybe you buried some of the nuts you collected during your former visits and you can find them again."

"I think this storm's going to blow over soon," Fire said. "Let's rest until the snow stops falling. Then we can go to the lady's cottage."

"Here, Squirrel. You can stay safe with me," Travis said, holding open his jacket. Squirrel climbed into a warm hiding place. Feeling hungry, he didn't expect to fall sleep easily.

*

Sometime later, Squirrel heard Baldwin's voice. "Sleeping friends, wake up! I've got news from Wings. He saw the old lady who wears purple shoes waking around the old mailbox. She was talking to herself about the boy's father and the need to fix things. Wings says something important is about to happen. The sun's out, and the snow has stopped. We're supposed to go to the mailbox right now."

"The magic mailbox!" yelled Travis, sitting up. "I wonder if my dad got my letter. We've got to go find him!"

"Baldwin, go back up the tree," Roar ordered. "Tell Wings that we're leaving right now. Everyone, follow me. I'm still king of this pride. It's time to reunite Travis with his father."

Chapter 19

A Father's Dream

*There is nothing sweeter in this sad world than the sound
of someone you love calling your name.*

—Kate DiCamillo, *The Tale of Despereaux*

Thomas set aside the files he had been working on and picked up his phone. He entered his code and checked emails and calls. Nothing from his wife, yet he didn't expect any messages after their last conversation. He hoped she would eventually understand his decision to stay at work instead of traveling to his mother's home for the holidays. He had many clients who needed attention.

He rubbed his eyes, thinking about their situation. Though Anne contributed to the family's finances through her part-time employment, he still felt responsible for paying the bills. He had to keep his present position in the law firm until he found another job that required fewer hours. He didn't want to share his search efforts with her until he had a definite offer. There was no choice but to work through the holidays, but he missed his family.

Memories of previous holidays filled his mind. Travis yelling with delight when he saw the gifts under the Christmas tree. The scents of Anne's cinnamon rolls baking in the oven and her smile when he played seasonal songs on the piano he had inherited from his great-grandmother. Lately, it seemed as though there were too few of these happy times with his family.

He tried pushing away his sadness and growing fatigue as he laid his head on his desk. "What am I supposed to do now with Anne and Travis caught in a snowstorm?" he murmured as he fell asleep and tumbled into another world.

*

Thomas squinted in the sunlight that spilled across the snow-covered field. He lifted his briefcase and adjusted the shoulder strap. It felt heavier than usual. He zipped up his coat, pulled gloves from his pocket, and started walking. Soon he passed a sign saying "The Path," with an arrow pointing away from the direction in which he was headed. He wondered if he was going in the correct direction, but there didn't seem to be another choice.

After he moved past the sign, he came upon a gravel road he recognized from his boyhood adventures on the White River. But something very strange caught his attention. A fork had been inserted into one of the posts on the side of the road where it split into two footpaths near a mailbox. It was an ordinary metal fork used to eat a meal.

"There you are, my dear boy."

Thomas turned toward the sound of the gentle voice. An old woman stood in the middle of the road, staring at him. She wore a thick blue jacket, red mittens, and old jeans. White hair fell loose onto her shoulders. Her eyes sparkled with the hue of goddess wisdom, and her radiant face, mostly free of wrinkles, shone with affection. He glanced down at her feet. In spite of the snow, the woman wore purple running shoes like his mother wore when he was a child.

"Mother?" he said. "I must be dreaming."

"Everything's a dream," she said. "I've missed you."

Thomas reached out his hands and tried to move toward her, wanting to touch her. But his feet were stuck in the ice.

"It's a marvelous December day," she said. "After the blizzard, we're lucky to have this sunshine. Perhaps we'll have a white Christmas this year after all."

"Mom, what are we doing here?"

"I'd like for you to look at this fork stuck in the post," she said. Her breath was visible in the cool air.

"I just noticed it. I was wondering why someone would put a fork right where the path split in two directions. And I remember that mailbox out here in the middle of the field. Didn't we collect clover together here during the summer?"

"Did you see the path sign?" his mother asked, pointing to the road behind him.

"Yeah, Mom, I saw it. But the arrow was pointing in the opposite direction from this place."

His mother's eyebrows arched as a hawk landed on a branch in a nearby tree. "Of course, my dear son. It's pointing in a different direction from the way you're traveling. Perhaps you're following a path created by others. You're certainly working too hard."

"What am I supposed to do? I need to support my family, and I want to give my son the things I didn't have as a boy after my father died."

"If it were my life," his mother said, "I would consider the options symbolized by the fork in the road. But first, let's look at what you really missed as a boy. I can assure you it wasn't things. Come here to the mailbox."

Thomas lifted his feet, surprised they were no longer stuck. He kicked through a pile of snow, unearthing autumn leaves. Then he followed his mother to the edge of the road where the mailbox was anchored on a shiny wood post. Thomas wondered if someone had recently painted it. It sparkled like a polished silver dollar, and the red flag was up.

"Do you remember the games we played with this old mailbox?" his mother asked.

"Yeah, it was a magic mailbox. But I'm grown up now, and there's no such thing as magic."

"But you're wrong. Open it and recover your magic. There's a boy waiting to be remembered."

Thomas hesitated, then reached for the latch. "What could it hurt?"

When he opened the door, a violet light spilled from the interior. Feeling uneasy, he extended a trembling hand into the box and pulled out a photo. Holding it up to his eyes, he saw a picture of his father and himself as a young boy. His throat tightened.

In the photo, he was standing on the banks of the White River, grasping a fishing pole. His father, Jay, stood behind him, his arms wrapped around his shoulders. Thomas remembered feeling his father's rough hands covering his small ones as they held the pole's handle together. Then how together, father and son, they dropped the lure into the slow-moving current where fish were swimming.

The photo faded, and other images took its place, one by one: Jay helping Thomas learn to ride a bike on the driveway in front of their first house. Jay taking him to the park and pushing the swing as Thomas screamed, "Higher! Push it higher!" Thomas sitting in his father's lap, sharing a bowl of popcorn while watching *Sesame Street* on a black-and-white TV. Thomas helping his father hang colored lights and silver tinsel on a Christmas tree. And finally, he saw his seven-year-old self, sitting next to his mother as the final words were spoken at his father's funeral.

Thomas clutched the photo in his hand, unable to speak.

"What you missed in your life was more of a relationship with your father," his mother said. "Not the stuff you think your son wants."

Thomas felt his eyes fill with tears as he met his mother's gaze. "I know, Mom, I know."

The sparkle disappeared from his mother's eyes, and wrinkles formed over her brow. "I have a memory that you were too young to remember. It's my holiday gift to you." She reached into the mailbox and withdrew another photo. "Look at this picture," she said, handing it to him. "You'll see what really mattered to your father when you were born."

Thomas stared at the photo of a brick cottage with a mature oak tree in the front yard. A young woman with long blonde hair stood in the driveway next to a convertible sports car. She held in her arms a baby wrapped in a blue blanket.

"There's a story about this photo," his mother continued. "Look closer."

The image shifted as though he were watching a video. A man took the baby from the woman. Cradling it gently, he walked to the trunk of the old oak and held him up toward the leafy branches.

"Welcome to the human race, little buddy," the man said. "I want to introduce you to our guardian tree. Thomas, this is Tree. Tree, this is Thomas, my precious newborn son. I love him very much, and I ask you to protect him and our home. Nothing will ever be more important than my family."

Thomas stood in silence, stunned by the love that he felt from his father's words. He turned toward his mother as the photos disappeared from his hands. "Thank you for this vision, Mom. It changes everything."

"That's why there's a fork in your road, Thomas. You have a choice to make. Are you going to continue on the path defined by false ideas about what's important or will you be the hero in your son's life?"

"I know which path I'll take," Thomas said as his mother vanished in a cloud of snowflakes.

In the next moment, Travis emerged from a row of frost-covered trees holding a squirrel in his hands. The backpack Thomas had given his son last Christmas hung over the boy's shoulder. A circle of animals gathered around the boy as he lifted his arm and waved.

Thomas called out, "Travis, it's me, your father."

"I see you!" Travis yelled, trekking through the snow in his direction.

Thomas held out his arms to his son, wanting to hug him. "I've missed you so much."

Travis stopped a few feet from his father, frowning. Snow swirled between them. "Dad, did you get my letter? I mailed it in that mailbox."

Thomas turned and looked at the magic mailbox. "What letter?"

*

"Wake up, Tom."

Thomas sat up, trying to make sense of the young law clerk standing over him. "Ross, I must have fallen asleep."

"Yes, and dreaming too. You were talking and reaching for that photo on your desk."

Thomas glanced at the framed picture of him as a boy, fishing with his father on the White River. He picked up the picture. "It's really interesting how we can be surrounded by memories and forget the importance of them sitting right in front of us."

"I came upstairs to give you something," Ross said. "I've been clearing out the mail, and there's a letter for you. Special delivery. It's a good thing I was here to sign for it. It must be very important. Looks like a kid's writing."

Thomas set the picture down and took the letter in his hands. "Yes, it's from Travis. It *is* important. Ross, go home and spend the holidays with your family. Neither of us needs to be here during Christmas. I've got a plane to catch."

Chapter 20

Are We There Yet?

> You have been my friend. That in
> itself is a tremendous thing.
>
> —E. B. White, *Charlotte's Web*

Travis pushed his way past sleepy-eyed travelers pulling wheeled bags through the entrance into the Philadelphia International Airport. He had his sights set on the moving walkway that would take him to terminal F and the security checkpoint.

"Mom, this is so much fun!" he exclaimed. Grabbing the rubber handhold of the walkway, he leaped behind a woman dragging a yellow, oversized duffel bag.

"Be careful, Travis," his mother warned. "Stand to your right and keep your backpack out of the way of people who are walking past us. Everyone is in a hurry today. I'm glad we finally got a flight that will get us to Indianapolis in time for Christmas. It's been two long days waiting for the storm to pass."

"I can't wait to get to Grandma's house and see Riverwood

Hollow," Travis said. "I dreamed about Daddy last night. He was there."

"That sounds like a lovely dream. I wish it were true."

As they approached the terminal, an automated voice caught Travis's attention. "The moving walkway is coming to an end. Please watch your step." Travis jumped off the walkway and pulled his backpack higher on his shoulder.

After arriving at the security checkpoint, they removed their shoes and coats. His mother took her computer out of her bag. She deposited it along with her coat and shoes into two gray plastic bins and set them on the conveyer belt moving through an x-ray machine. Travis set his coat and shoes into one of the bins.

He was about to place his backpack on the conveyor belt when a security agent standing next to the body scan machine yelled, "Hey, kid, what's that animal in your bag?"

Travis saw the man's alarmed expression as he approached the stack of bins. Without thinking, Travis blurted, "He's my pet squirrel. He travels in my backpack."

A young woman with purple hair standing behind him added, "Yeah … it's the kid's totem animal." The woman burst out laughing, and Travis put his hands over his mouth, trying to muffle his own giggling.

The agent put his hands on his hips. "It's no laughing matter," he said. "I thought it was a real animal. Young man, you will have to remove your stuffy from the bag and put it through the machine separately." Wiping perspiration from a shiny bald head, he moved to a place on the opposite side of the body scan machine, where he stood with crossed arms.

"But that's crazy," Travis whispered to the young woman, while catching a glimpse of the agent's stare.

"It's fine, Travis," his mother said, touching his shoulder. "Everyone's a bit on edge today. Let's just flow with it."

Travis sighed. "OK, Mom." He thought it best to avoid trying to reason with a security person who looked like one of the villains in a superhero movie. Noticing the frown on his mother's face, he knew better than to argue with her.

After placing Squirrel in one of the containers, he set it on the conveyor belt along with the bin holding his coat, shoes, and backpack. He thought he saw a smile spread across the puppet's face as he passed out of sight beneath the x-ray machine.

When Travis and his mother arrived at the departure gate

designated for Indianapolis, they settled into the molded black seats in the row nearest the counter.

Exhaling a long breath, his mother reached into her bag and pulled out her phone. "Let's call your dad," she said, punching in his number. A few seconds later, she turned off the phone. "That's strange. He said he'd talk to both of us before we boarded the plane. You were asleep when he called last night. I didn't want to wake you."

As his mother returned the phone to her bag, the agent behind the counter picked up the microphone. "Attention, passengers waiting for American Eagle flight 4520 to Indianapolis. We are going to hold up boarding due to an unexpected repair."

"Oh dear," Anne said. "Squirrel energy strikes again. I hope we'll get out of this airport sometime today."

An hour later, they boarded their flight. When they approached their assigned seats, his mother pointed to the window seat. "Travis, sit next to the window this time so you can see the Indianapolis skyline from the air when we begin to land."

Once the plane had taken off, Travis turned toward his mother. "Mom, what's a totem animal? That purple-haired woman in line at the security check point said Squirrel was my totem animal."

"Great question. According to some people, a totem animal is a special ally or friend. Remember the animals you saw on the puppet tree back in the gift shop? From all those animals, you probably chose the squirrel because you sensed a connection to him, like he was meant to be your ally or friend."

"So, Squirrel is my totem animal?" Travis asked.

Anne shifted in her seat. "Not really. I'll try to explain it. Some Native Americans believe each person is born into a family or a clan that is associated with a specific bird or animal, like the wolf clan, bear clan, or turtle clan. That animal is the totem for a specific Native American family or community."

Travis frowned. "So Squirrel is not my totem animal?"

"Let me clarify. Many people have borrowed the idea of a totem animal and changed its original meaning. When a person says he has a totem animal, he really means he has a spirit animal. Like I said, a friend, ally, or helper. A spirit animal may show up in a person's dream or in some meaningful experience during everyday life. Then the person forms a relationship with his spirit animal. That spirit animal helps protect the person or gives him important guidance or assistance when needed. Spirit animals are sometimes called power animals. But a person's spirit animal is not necessarily related to the family or clan in which one is born."

"I'm not sure why, but there's something about squirrels I like. Maybe because they climb trees and run around in the woods."

"And the squirrel is playful like you," his mother said. "We all have special relationships with certain animals or birds and are attracted to the qualities of those creatures. Like the owl's wisdom or its ability to see in the dark."

"Do grown-up people have spirit animals too? Not just us kids?"

"That's right. My main spirit animal is the hawk."

"I think I get it," Travis said. "You've said sometimes you can see things that others can't when you take your photographs. Maybe the hawk's vision helps you."

"Yes, I think you've got the idea. Sometimes I ask my spirit animal for help to see something different about a situation in everyday life too. Most of the time, I receive the guidance I need—like learning from your trickster squirrel how to be flexible when our planes have been delayed and cancelled."

"I bet it's important to have a close friendship with your spirit animal or helper," Travis said.

"That's right. And relationships take time to develop. When you have a scary dream or nightmare, you can call up a spirit animal as a guardian. That raccoon hero from your favorite movies would be a great ally to keep close when you fall asleep. You can have more than one spirit animal friend."

"Thanks, Mom. I think I'll read a story on my tablet before we land." Travis opened his tablet, but it was hard to focus on the story he had been reading. He thought more about his spirit animal, wondering if Squirrel could help bring his father to Grandma's house for Christmas like what had happened in his dream.

*

Squirrel had been listening to the conversation between Travis and his mother. He was glad to know about spirit animals and was determined to be the best spirit animal possible for his boy. Now that they were finally flying to Indianapolis, Squirrel hoped he could find his way back to his friends in the snowy dream world. He wanted to be an ally to Travis, but he also wanted to help his own puppet family.

Chapter 21

The Best Gift Ever

Why, sometimes I've believed as many as
six impossible things before breakfast.

—Lewis Carroll, *Through the Looking-*
Glass, and What Alice Found There

Travis stared out the window as the plane flew past the tall buildings in downtown Indianapolis and descended toward the airport. The city and its surrounding neighborhoods sprawled over the landscape for what seemed like miles. He spotted the Indianapolis Motor Speedway oval track, remembering when he last made a trip to his grandmother's house. His dad was with him then and had pointed out the landmark. He had promised to take him to the 500 Mile Race. Travis wondered if it would ever happen when his dad couldn't even get to Indianapolis for Christmas.

Once the plane landed and came to a full stop, the other passengers stood up and opened the overhead compartments. While talking into smartphones, they pulled out carry-on suitcases and shopping bags full of gifts. Travis watched his mother reach for her tote bag beneath the seat in front of her and then noticed tears in her eyes.

"We'll sit here until everyone else gets off the plane," she said, wiping a hand across her cheeks. "We're not in a rush. No one will be waiting for us in the airport. I told Grandma Floi that we'd get a cab from the airport. With the weather still unpredictable, I wasn't sure when we would finally make it to Indianapolis. We'll try to call your dad once we get our checked luggage from the baggage claim area. I don't know where he could have been when I tried to call this morning."

Travis didn't know what to say. He looked down at the squirrel tucked under his arm, thinking about the dreams he had while at the hotel in Philadelphia. It had been confusing to travel in both the dream world and his regular life and keep things straight in his mind. So he sat quietly in his seat, watching passengers move down the aisle toward the front of the plane. He worried about his dad and hoped to talk to him. He wanted to know what happened to the letter.

When most of the passengers had exited the plane, Travis pulled the backpack out from under his seat and stuffed the squirrel into the top compartment. "There you are, Squirrel. We're in Indianapolis now, where my grandma lives."

Travis followed his mother down the terminal's corridor into the central waiting area. Looking up at the colossal ceiling and around at the assortment of shops and cafes, he adjusted his backpack, pushing both arms through the shoulder straps. When he caught the odor of fries cooking and the scent of the fresh-brewed coffee his mother liked, he wondered when they could get something to eat. The only snack served on the flight had been a tiny bag of pretzels.

Once they had descended the escalator and reached the baggage claim area on the lower level, Anne pointed to the right. "This way for the American Airlines carousel."

Travis looked up at his mother's face. She was frowning like she often did when having to make a decision. "What's wrong, Mom?"

"Nothing you need to worry about. I'm looking for the car rental counters. Then I'll try to call your dad again." All at once, she stopped and dropped her carry-on bag. "Thomas!"

Travis turned just before his father lifted him off the floor and pulled his mother into a hug. Feeling the strength of his father's arms, Travis dropped his head against his shoulder. His parents stood pressed together for a long time before Travis felt his feet on the floor again.

"I was worried when you didn't get off the plane right away," his father said. "I thought I had missed you somehow or you hadn't made this flight."

"This is a surprise! I can't believe it!" Anne exclaimed, wiping the tears from her eyes.

"I wanted to pick you guys up," Thomas said. "You've been through so much with the snowstorm."

"But how did you get here before us?" Anne asked.

"I had a dream about Travis, and then I received his letter by special delivery. I realized I needed to be with my family. I rushed to the airport and managed to catch two flights that got me here before you guys arrived."

Travis wrapped his arms around his father's waist. "Oh, Daddy, I'm so glad you're here. I missed you, and I have so much to tell you."

"I have a surprise to share with you too," Thomas said. "There'll be time for us to talk later. I couldn't let my family celebrate Christmas without me. I love you too much to stay home and work."

"I love you too, Daddy. And now we'll be together. It's the best Christmas gift ever."

"I rented a car and parked it in the garage," Thomas said. "Let's get your luggage first. Then we'll stop for lunch at Ruthie's Sunshine Café on the way to my mom's house. There's quite a story to tell. Right now, I'm relieved you arrived in Indianapolis safely."

*

Hearing the words about love spoken between Travis and his father, Squirrel quivered with excitement. Now he wondered about his friends in the dream world. Was it possible love could reunite them? This question swirled around in Squirrel's mind as he drifted to sleep.

Squirrel found his way to the field where he had first seen wildflowers, dragonflies, and the old lady wearing purple running shoes. This time, he found a field of melting snow and his friends huddled around a firepit. Smoke rose above orange flames. The dragon stood watch over the fire. Wings was perched on a branch in a nearby apple tree, and Roar was crouched next to Pinkie, his head resting on his front paws. Squirrel scampered through the snow toward the warmth of the fire. The animals turned in Squirrel's direction when he stopped in front of Roar.

"You won't believe what happened in the boy's world!" Squirrel exclaimed, standing upright and waving his paws. "His father flew into Indianapolis and picked his mother and him up at the airport. We're all going to his grandmother's house."

Roar stood up and paced back and forth in front of the rest of the circle. Then he dropped down beneath the apple tree, shaking his mane as though tossing off troublesome thoughts. Turning toward Squirrel, he said, "The last time we saw you and the boy was when he called out to his father standing next to that magic mailbox. Then both of you disappeared. It seems like the rest of us are stuck in this place."

"What's going to happen to us?" Pinkie asked. "I don't know what to do about these babies, and I just found another one clinging to my left side. I don't understand where they're all coming from."

"You're a wonderful mother," Roar said, petting her head.

The dragon blew fire into a log that had nearly gone out before speaking. "Maybe there's a way we all can get from this world into the boy's world. Perhaps we can dream ourselves there in the same way we dreamed our way here."

Bandita dipped her paws into a puddle of slushy snow and licked the moisture dripping from her claws. "How's that possible if we're stuck here?"

"Well," Roar began, "I think it's a matter of intention. If our intention to travel to the boy's world is strong enough, then it might be possible. Fire taught us how to do it before, and we were successful getting here when we wanted to be with Squirrel. Yet there's something we're not thinking of. Some part of the puzzle is missing."

Wings nodded his head from the branch in the apple tree. "I know one thing. We can't travel back to the gift shop. I'm not sure why I know this, but it's simply not possible."

The dragon spit more fire onto the logs. Bandita and Pinkie dragged another one from the pile at the base of the apple tree. "I agree with you, Wings," Fire said. "I sense our puppet bodies are trapped in a place between the worlds, but maybe there's a chance we can dream our way out of it, like Roar said."

Shelltin frowned. "I don't understand a word of what you guys are talking about. All I know for certain is that we're near Turtle Alley. It's on the other side of this frozen field."

Squirrel leaned under the turtle's shell and faced him. "At least with the dragon's fire, it's warm enough for you to stick out your head and hear what's going on."

"Being together is what really matters," Roar said, scratching his mane. "So, if there's a way out of here, I'll find it and take us all home … wherever that might be."

"What about the boy?" Bandita asked. "Will we ever see him again?"

Each of the animals fell silent, gazing at the fire while the dragon continued to feed it with hot flames streaming from his mouth. Squirrel slipped away from the fire ring, wondering if Roar could lead his friends out of the snowy realm where they were trapped.

Chapter 22

A New Dream

So, what do you do with a chance?
You take it … because it just might be
the start of something incredible.

—Kobi Yamada, *What Do You Do with a Chance?*

Travis opened the tiny box of crayons and sketched a picture of a mailbox on the back of the children's menu. He would never forget the story about the magic mailbox and how the letter to his father had been delivered to the law office. He didn't really want to color a picture of a silly rooster standing next to a barn; he was more interested in the surprise his father wanted to share. While he waited for his father to break the silence that had fallen over the table, he scanned the café. The yellow walls were covered with old photographs and signs. Displayed in a cabinet behind where he sat were stacks of yellow T-shirts printed with the café's name.

"Ruthie's Sunshine Café was always my favorite place to eat," Thomas said. "Travis, your grandmother used to bring me here when I was a kid. I'm glad to see it's stayed in business. And it's just across the bridge from your grandmother's cottage on the White River. Hey, I bet you'd like the Mickey Mouse pancake. It's still on the menu."

Travis groaned. His father hadn't noticed how much he'd changed during the past few months. He wasn't a little boy anymore, and now he wondered if his father remembered his upcoming birthday, just after Christmas. Maybe it was the stuffed squirrel puppet he carried with him that made him seem like a little kid. But Squirrel was more than a toy. He was his spirit animal.

"Ah, Dad, I think I'll have the French toast sticks."

"Great choice," Thomas said. "I'm glad you found something you like. As soon as we order, I'd like to share my news with you."

When the server came to their table to take their orders, Anne shifted in her seat. "I'm not quite sure what to get. Why don't you two go first. There are so many wonderful choices."

"Well," said Thomas, "I'll have the special meat omelet, fried potatoes, and coffee, black."

Travis dropped the crayon, wanting to look mature. "I'll have hot chocolate with whipped cream and the French toast sticks. Oh, and a small orange juice."

Anne sighed. "For me, the vegetable scramble with fruit and green tea."

Thomas raised his eyebrows. "Anne, it's not like you to pass on a good cup of coffee for green tea."

"I also have some news to share," Anne said, pushing a lock of hair behind her ear. "But I'd love for you to tell us your news before I share mine."

Thomas took a deep breath. "Anne, I haven't been totally honest with you."

"I know something's been bothering you," Anne replied, glancing at Travis. "Is this a conversation we should be having now?"

Thomas smiled. "Yes, my news is for both of you. I've been looking for a different job. For the past couple months, I've been sending out résumés and interviewing by phone with smaller law firms, most in the Indianapolis area. I've wanted a job with a firm that doesn't require so many hours of work that it takes me away from you all the time. But I had to keep working long hours until something else showed up."

Anne unwrapped her napkin from the silverware and set it in her lap. "Why Indianapolis?"

"We both grew up in Indianapolis," Thomas replied. "My mother lives here, and the cost of living is much less than the West Coast."

"So why didn't you tell me?" Anne asked, taking a drink of water.

"Because I didn't want to address the possibility until I actually had an offer. And I know how much you've loved the Seattle area."

"Dad, do you have an offer?" Travis asked.

"Yes. Before I picked you up from the airport, I got a phone call. It's an offer from a small firm that is family friendly and supports the arts in Indianapolis. I had a personal interview with them a couple of weeks ago when I came to Indianapolis to check on your grandmother. The salary is not quite as high as I was making in Seattle, but houses are less expensive here. They want me to start after the holidays."

"Wow, that's short notice," Anne said as her eyes filled with tears.

"Anne, I'm really sorry to spring it on you all at once. It's just that I am really excited about this opportunity."

"I was worried your news might be bad news."

"I didn't want to accept the offer until I discussed it with you and Travis," Thomas said, pausing when the server brought their breakfast orders.

Travis felt nervous about moving, but if it meant he could have more time with his dad, he thought it was a good idea. He waited until the server left and then leaned over the table toward his father. "Dad, are you going to take the job?"

"I'm waiting to hear how your mother feels. We're a team."

"Mom, what do you think about moving?"

Anne smiled and looked at Thomas first, then back toward Travis. "This is good news for all of us. I like the idea of moving back to Indianapolis. There are several reasons why it's a good idea. I have many friends who still live in the area, and your cousins Greyson and Kristen have a home in Carmel, just north of Indianapolis. You'll have so much fun living close to your grandma and playing in her sanctuary next to the river. I love being close to family." She paused before turning toward Thomas. "Also, when I was younger, I always dreamed of attending the Herron School of Art and Design."

Thomas set his coffee cup down. "Then I'll accept the position. Anne, I'm glad you aren't angry that I kept this from you. You said you had something important to share too. Do you want to tell us now?"

Anne wiped her eyes with her napkin. "Recently, I learned something that will also change our lives," she said, pausing to take a breath. "Travis is going to have a baby brother or sister. Thomas, I'm pretty excited but was nervous about sharing the news. I didn't know how you'd feel. I've waited a while to tell you, wanting to make sure it would be the right time. Now feels like that time. It'll be wonderful to be near your mother when the baby is born."

Thomas reached across the table and took his wife's hands in his. "I love you very much, and this news makes me happy for all of us."

"I won't be an only child anymore," Travis said, jumping up to hug his dad. "And you're going to have time to help me with my math homework … and take me fishing. My spirit animal is happy, too, because a dream has come true. We're going to be together as a family at Christmas."

"And it's a perfect birthday present for my talented son who is growing up. It's hard to believe you'll be eleven in two weeks."

Chapter 23

The Box between the Worlds

It was confusing the way the idea of impossible
things kept tumbling into the real world.

—Charles de Lint, *The Cats of Tanglewood Forest*

Roar scratched the fur that had thickened around his neck and head. "It's the mane of a lion!" he exclaimed. Pushing his nose against a cardboard wall, he realized he was no longer a cat sitting on snowy ground around a fire ring in Squirrel's dream world.

"Roar, is that your tail in my mouth?" a voice called from beneath a layer of plastic on which he was sitting.

"I hear you, Bandita, but I'm trying to figure out where I am," replied Roar.

"You mean where *we* are," called another voice Roar recognized as Fire's.

Several groans erupted from within what seemed to be a small space. Roar had been in this situation before. He reasoned that each of the puppets was wrapped in a plastic cover and piled on top of one another. Then they were packed among what humans called peanuts, which were not things that could be eaten. He was on top of the pile. He liked that, feeling it was his rightful place.

He slumped down farther into the plastic. He remembered the stuff from the first time he had been packed in a box. He would never forget the way the clerk had lifted him out of the box and unrolled him from what he came to understand was bubbly wrap. "You're a cool puppet, so handsome," she had said to him as she looked into his eyes and stroked his mane.

Throughout his adventures in Riverwood Hollow, Roar had tried to maintain his self-image. During the days when he lived in the gift shop, he had been respected by the other animals that had looked to him for leadership. They had depended upon him to protect their tree of life, and he had taken his responsibility seriously. But somehow, the loss of his thick mane and becoming an ordinary cat had eroded his position of authority. The qualities that defined him as a courageous and wise king had been seized by the hawk and dragon. Now it was time to fully reclaim his proper place in their family as their true leader.

His first order of business was to figure out what was happening. He already had a clue from the discussion at the fire ring. Wings and Fire had talked about not being able to go back to the gift shop. If he was now a lion puppet and not a cat, then they were no longer in the squirrel's dream world. And if they weren't in the gift shop, then they must be in another place in the waking world.

"That's it!" he exclaimed, pawing his eyes.

"That's what, Lion?" said a voice Roar knew belonged to the opossum.

"We're packed in sheets of protective plastic, and we're in a box being shipped somewhere," Roar said.

A rumble of voices rose to the top of the pile as Roar struggled to free himself from the sticky plastic that had been taped over his front paws.

"I'm where?" a voice chittered.

"Squirrel?" Roar called.

"No, it's me Baldwin, the other squirrel."

"How did you end up here with us?" Roar asked.

"I'm not sure. I was plucked out of a window display where I've been sitting in a corner for years. I think it was part of a gift shop where there were lots of people waiting for planes. A long time ago, I got bored and since then have spent my days in a wooded place next to a river."

"Yes, I remember you, big Baldwin," a voice screeched. "My puppet self is feeling a bit hungry right now."

"Wings, you can't eat someone whose name you know," Baldwin barked. "Besides, I bet your puppet self would not be able to digest me."

Roar growled. "We have more pressing issues to solve. Like … ah … where we're going. Wings, don't let your feathers get ruffled, and keep your talons to yourself."

"I'm hearing everyone's voices above me," yelled Shelltin. "I must be buried beneath the rest of you, and I can't stick my head out far enough to see anything."

"I smell smoke, and I've lost my babies!" screamed Pinkie.

"Fire, you've got to control yourself," the lion roared. "We're in a confined space."

"Oh, that's right, now you're in charge," replied Fire. "I was just trying to shed some light on the situation. How do you know what's happening?"

"Think about it, Fire," Roar said. "You're the expert on magic. You know about the dream world. You and Wings knew we couldn't go back to the gift shop from where we ended up at the fire ring. But I've figured out something else. Try to remember when you were first shipped to the gift shop. We were together in that shipment, wrapped in the same kind of plastic wrap as we are now. We're no longer in Squirrel's dream world. We're in our waking world as puppets, able to talk and move because there are no humans nearby."

"I think you're right, Roar," Fire said. "This is just like that other time. We really are in a shipping box. I knew something was up when we talked at the fire ring, but I didn't imagine this situation."

"Where might we be going?" asked the turtle. "Being on what appears to be the bottom of the box, I feel like I'm holding up the rest of you on my back."

"Hey, I asked about my babies," screamed Pinkie. "I've lost them."

"Calm down, friends," Roar said, attempting to gently reassure the members of his kingdom. "Shelltin, your back is safe. According to many legends, you are fully capable of holding the entire world on your shell. Plus, there's lots of padding in this plastic. Pinkie, you had babies in the dream world. But you didn't have them in the gift shop world."

"So, we … we've been separated, and they … they've been left behind?" Pinkie whimpered.

Hearing her sobs, Roar reached out a paw and pushed aside the plastic. He wanted to reassure the opossum. He found her tail draped over his back leg. Grabbing the hairless tail, he gave it a slight tug. "Calm down, Pinkie. They were old enough to be on their own. I'm sure that once we figure everything out, you can find them again. We'll help you reunite with them in the future."

"I can't think about a future without them," Pinkie cried.

"If Roar is right about being in a box wrapped in this disgusting plastic," Wings said, "then there's one thing to be grateful about."

"What's that?" asked Roar, feeling his patience weaken.

"We're all together," said Wings.

"Except for Squirrel," added Baldwin.

"That's because we're a family," Roar said. He knew it was his job to keep the puppets feeling secure until they knew where they were being shipped. He understood how important his next words would be. So, he put aside his own fear about where they might be headed. "Like Wings just said, the main thing is the rest of us are in the same box. And I'll do everything possible to keep us together. You can count on me. I'll keep my promise. Oh, and one more thing. We're safe, if Fire doesn't smoke us out or burn us up."

"Thank you, Roar," said Bandita. "I always knew you had a heart."

"You're very welcome. I'm hopeful we'll also find Squirrel. In the meantime, listen to me. Close your eyes and imagine yourselves in another place, maybe Riverwood Hollow in summertime. Can you do that? Journey to your special dream place while things get sorted out in this shipping box and we are delivered to our destination. Tell me now, friends, where are you in your imagination?"

"I see them now!" Pinkie exclaimed. "My babies are on my back. Oh, happy day! I see flowers and lots of green, leafy trees with bugs to eat—and butterflies too."

"I'm plodding through the sandy paths in Turtle Alley," Shelltin said. "There are female turtles digging nests for their eggs."

"I hear the splatter of water where some of those turtles are swimming," said Bandita. "Did you guys know I can swim too?"

"I see a juicy chipmunk in a clover field," added Wings.

"I've dug out of the cave in the roots, and I'm flying into the clouds over the Great River Tree," said Fire.

"That's right. Keep dreaming of your special places," Roar said as he tapped the side of the box. "Listen to the beat of my paw."

*

Sometime later, Roar felt a thunderous impact as though the box had been dropped. Then the sound of a bell ringing, a door opening, and a woman's voice. "Wonderful! Just in time for Christmas."

"What was that?" asked Pinkie.

"I think we've arrived at our destination," Roar answered.

"Most likely another store," said Bandita.

"Have courage in your hearts," Roar said. He knew that Christmas was a time for miracles. After all, he was a lion, and he had journeyed in his imagination to their new home.

Chapter 24

Christmas Day

That night he was almost too happy to
sleep, and so much love stirred in his little
sawdust heart that it almost burst.

—Margery Williams, *The Velveteen Rabbit*

Travis caught the scents of bacon frying and cinnamon buns baking while still dreaming. Opening his eyes, he pulled the comforter up to his chin and looked out the window from his bed. The rising sun cast a shimmering light over a sycamore tree on the other side of the river path. A large hawk was perched on one of the snow-covered branches.

"Finally, it's Christmas!" he said, smiling at the memory of his father showing up at the airport. The news he would finally have a brother or sister had been another welcome surprise. Being an only child had been tough, and he hoped to tell the new baby stories he'd written about Riverwood Hollow. Leaping out of bed, he grabbed a sweater and slipped it over his superhero pajamas. Taking Squirrel from his pillow, he raced to the living room.

The Christmas tree sparkled with strings of little white lights and a collection of homemade ornaments. For a long moment, Travis stood there, gasping in disbelief. Beneath the tree, dressed in shiny ribbons and bows, sat the animal puppets that he and Squirrel had left at the gift shop in the Seattle-Tacoma International Airport.

Speechless, he dropped down to the holiday blanket surrounding the tree. The opossum, lion, hawk, raccoon, and turtle were all there. Next to them sat another squirrel puppet, bigger than the puppet Travis carried in his arms. Travis thought they looked like a family all dressed up for the holidays.

When his mother, father, and grandmother entered the room, he exclaimed, "Mom! Dad! Grandma! Santa brought me Squirrel's friends."

Anne smiled. "Santa has a way of knowing just what a boy wants."

"A squirrel needs his friends just like a boy needs his family," Thomas said. "A mother and a father."

"What about a grandmother?" Floi said.

Travis ran to his grandmother and gave her a hug. "You're always part of our family," he said.

Anne pulled a dragon puppet from behind her back. "Travis, I almost forgot. There's one more puppet. I found this one lying in the corner of the shipping box as I was removing all the wrappings."

"Mom, he's so cool! You're like one of Santa's elves."

"Santa told me that the poor dragon had been dropped into the return box just before we purchased the squirrel. Santa said he looked so sad. He couldn't resist adding him to the group."

"How could Santa have known that he's Squirrel's friend too?" Travis knew his mother had a big influence on Santa's Christmas gift decisions, but he didn't want to let her know how much he understood about Santa. After all, magic was magic, no matter how it happened.

Anne lifted the tag on the dragon's neck. "Look," she said. "His name is Fire."

Travis took the dragon in his arms. Lifting his wings, he examined the spot where a hand could make them move. "I love him. There's been a dragon in my dreams. He's been part of the story I'm writing."

Anne's blue eyes sparkled with an expression Travis had seen many times. "Yes, a dream has a way of spilling into our everyday life," she said, glancing at Thomas.

Travis examined the tags of each puppet. "Just like Fire, all the right names: Roar, Wings, Bandita, Pinkie, and Shelltin. I remember seeing each of them on the puppet tree when Squirrel and I said goodbye to them. And they've been in my dreams."

Then he picked up the big squirrel and looked at the tag. "His name is Baldwin. I don't remember him on the puppet tree, but his name sounds familiar. Like from a dream. He must be one of Squirrel's best friends."

"According to Santa, he'd been sitting in a display in the gift shop window for a long time," his mom said. "I felt sorry for him, all alone without a family, especially now."

Travis hugged the two squirrels together with Fire. "I'll put these guys with their friends while you, Dad, and Grandma open your gifts."

*

Joining the other puppets under the Christmas Tree, Squirrel felt the familiar ache in his chest stronger than ever. With affection, he looked at each of his friends with whom he had shared many adventures. Fire grinned, his red tongue moving ever so slightly. Squirrel could imagine him saying, "I might have to blow a bit of smoke on this Christmas tree."

The hawk flipped his right wing, and his eyes glowed with

excitement. "I'd like to replace the angel at the top of this tree," he whispered.

Shelltin, Pinkie, and Bandita gazed at Squirrel with glistening eyes. Baldwin winked and said, "I will always be your princely friend."

"All of us together again with our tree of life, this time in Indianapolis," Roar said, as he fluffed his thick mane.

Squirrel finally understood what love meant. It was more than a feeling. It was knowing these animals were not just his friends. They were his true family, and all of them belonged together, no matter which world they lived in.

*

Later that morning, the doorbell rang. Travis rushed to the door, wondering who it could be. When he opened the door, a girl with long blonde hair, dressed in a red coat, looked down at him with a wide smile. She was clutching gift bags with curly ribbons tied to the handles.

"Kristen, you've grown taller," Travis said. "For a minute, I didn't recognize my own cousin."

"It's time to open presents!" shouted a younger boy dressed in a trendy ski jacket.

"Greyson, try to be polite," Kristen said as Travis's younger cousin pushed his way through the entrance hall toward the Christmas tree.

Travis thought about how he and Greyson were the same age yet so different. Greyson was more athletic and sported a cropped haircut that fit his energetic personality.

Uncle Ken held up a large box of wrapped presents, and his wife, Brianna, carried a platter of cookies. Travis's aunt and uncle wore matching Christmas sweaters, and their faces glowed a rosy shade of pink from the cold weather.

Anne approached the open door. "It's been way too long since we've been together for the holidays," she said. "And we've got so much to catch up on."

Before lunch, Travis's family exchanged gifts. Anne gave *The Jungle Book* purchased in the gift shop to Travis and the book about Norse mythology to Greyson. To Kristen, who was an avid reader, she gave *The Chronicles of Narnia.* She kept *The Velveteen Rabbit,* Beatrice Potter's *The Complete Tales,* and a stuffed bunny for her new baby.

Thomas gave each of the children Lego sets based upon recent movies. Travis received a box of colored art pencils and a sketch pad from his cousins. Seeing smiles on everyone's faces and hearing the excitement over the new baby, Travis knew that being with family during the holidays was his best gift.

*

After the day had ended and his parents and grandmother were asleep, Travis slipped out of bed and tiptoed in stocking feet back to the Christmas tree. He picked up one of the books his mother kept for the new baby and gathered up all the puppets in his arms. He carried his puppet family back to his little bedroom and set them together on the antique iron bed. Hugging Squirrel next to his chest, Travis opened *The Velveteen Rabbit* and read the story to him.

"You'll always be like the Velveteen Rabbit to me, a real squirrel," Travis whispered before drifting to sleep.

Chapter 25

The Next Summer

And so for a time it looked as if all the adventures
were coming to an end; but that was not to be.

—C. S. Lewis, *The Lion, the Witch, and the Wardrobe*

The canopy of the forest sanctuary grew thick with early summer foliage. Only a trickle of light penetrated the tunnel of twined branches. Entering the field where he had first encountered the old woman, Squirrel noticed wildflowers and clover blanketing the area around the fire ring. Everything looked different from the snow-covered place in the dreams he'd had before Christmas when he thought his family had been lost.

On the side of the gravel road, honeysuckle bushes dripped with moisture, and the scent of river water permeated the air. Tiny mushrooms cropped up on the sides of fallen branches untouched by the sun. Birds chirped from treetops. Squirrel remembered the feeling of freedom experienced during his adventures in the dream world.

On this morning, Travis's grandmother drove three children and his puppet family in a specially designed golf cart through Riverwood

Hollow. From his place on Travis's lap in the front passenger seat, Squirrel could keep up with the conversations and had a clear view of the sanctuary the old woman loved so much. He knew now that the woman in his dreams had been Travis's grandmother. Even today, she wore purple shoes. He'd learned from her long-winded lectures that many of the flowers, including ones called lilies, she had planted on the banks of the river when she was a young woman.

"I dreamed about this place," Travis said. "Even the gravel road and the pond. And there's the magic mailbox I told you guys about."

From the back seat, Kristen lifted up Fire, making his mouth move. "Let's open it and fire up a message on a map."

Greyson laughed. "Travis, I love that story about the map and your letter to Uncle Thomas."

As they circled the side of an algae-covered pond, Squirrel saw dragonflies buzzing the surface of the water and a blue heron wading along the shore. When they passed the sandy paths of Turtle Alley, where turtles were digging nests for their eggs, he glanced at Shelltin sitting on the dashboard. The turtle's eyes widened. Wings, who sat between Travis and his grandmother, looked up into the trees as though searching for a tiny bird to eat.

Pointing to one of the sycamore trees, Floi said, "Do you hear the tapping? Just like a drum calling you into the imaginal realm."

"I see it," Kristen said from the back seat. "It's a woodpecker."

"A pileated woodpecker," Greyson added, pointing toward the tree branch where Kristen was staring.

Travis turned toward the back seat with his hand inside Squirrel's mouth. "How do you know so much about this place?" he asked. Squirrel silently wished he could tell Greyson a thing or two about Riverwood Hollow.

Greyson held up Bandita, making her mouth move. "I've lived here all my life and have played in this area," he said in a high-pitched voice. Changing to his regular voice, he added, "By the way, I once saw a raccoon climbing Grandma's bird feeders. It slurped up all the seeds and nuts. It even drank the nectar from the hummingbird feeder. Last summer, I saw one swimming along the banks of the White River with a baby turtle in its mouth. I think the raccoon was going to eat it."

"Gross!" squealed Kristen. "I bet Shelltin wouldn't like that."

Floi stopped the golf cart. Squirrel noticed the sparkle in her eyes as she turned toward the children. "You kids will have several opportunities to play here this summer. Our new baby boy, Tobias, needs lots of care right now. Travis, your parents need extra rest because of his feeding schedule. You kids will stay with me during part of the summer. I know you'll have summer classes and athletic practices. But you can come here on the weekends, and I have sleeping bags."

"Maybe we can camp out in a tent too," Travis suggested.

"And maybe we can get bit by lots of bugs," Greyson said, tapping Travis on the head with the dragon's claw. "I'm glad you guys moved here, even if you have some goofy ideas."

"I'm glad to have human playmates. It's more fun than being an only child," Travis said. "You two are like my brother and sister."

Floi glanced at Travis. "Let's take a look at the rest of Riverwood Hollow. I want you children to know more about the White River." She started the golf cart and turned down a narrow path that Squirrel recognized. He remembered when the big squirrel saved him from a vicious dog and how Wings eyed big Baldwin as a juicy meal. He noticed Baldwin sitting in the back seat in Kristen's lap, as far away as possible from Wings.

Keeping her eyes on the path, Floi began talking again. "There are entire universes tucked inside this sanctuary. In the muck of the pond, there are water bugs that will become dragonflies. Among bushes, spiders create luminous webs, and within the deepest part of this forest, a deer nurses her fawn." Squirrel had nearly fallen asleep when the golf cart stopped again.

As Floi continued her lecture, it was impossible for Squirrel to miss her gleeful expression. "The forests in Indiana around the river are made up of many trees. They include maple, birch, hickory, walnut, sycamore, and several varieties of oaks. There are a couple special trees in this area. We're headed to a great sycamore at the end of the path. It's estimated to be hundreds of years old. Some say nearly four hundred. And there's a huge swamp chestnut oak deep in the woods we've already passed. According to a friend of mine, it was a small sapling when Indiana became a state in 1816. We'll see it on the way home."

"Oh, Grandma," Travis said, rolling his eyes. "Can't we just play in the woods without knowing the names and history of the trees?"

"Of course, dear, but there's so much to learn about this river environment. Like all the blue jays, gold finches, vultures, hawks, tree sparrows, red-winged blackbirds, cardinals, egrets, and herons, to name just a few. But most importantly, there's one thing I want you kids to do about the river's environment." With her last words, Floi began driving the golf cart toward the sound of splashing water.

"I know what it is," said Kristen, holding Pinkie in front of Squirrel. "I'm an opossum, and I'm the only North American marsupial. I eat lots of ticks and grubs and can kill snakes and rats. I'm nature's garbage collector, and I'm going to clean up this place. Look at me. I even carry babies on my back."

Squirrel remembered how Pinkie's babies had reappeared after the children acted out an imaginary story in the meadow near the apple tree. In their play, the opossum found some orphan babies next to the fire ring, and then like magic a couple days later, baby opossums dangled from her back. Squirrel suspected that Travis's grandmother had overheard the story and had something to do with the addition of the babies.

Kristen shook Pinkie, causing the babies to wiggle. "Did you know that opossums are immune to most snake venom, including rattlesnake bites?"

"There's a story about Rikki-Tikki-Tavi in *The Jungle Book* I'm reading," added Travis. "But the animal in the story is a mongoose. It removes a snake from a little boy's bedroom."

Floi parked the cart near the roots of a giant sycamore and pointed to the roots breaking the surface around its trunk. "This is where you kids will help that opossum, beginning right now."

Seeing the towering tree, Squirrel wanted to leap out of the golf cart. The shoreline looked like the Point. He remembered one of his dreams when the animals and Travis hid in a cave beneath the roots of the Great River Tree during a blizzard. Travis's story about the killing of a snake brought back the worst memory of that nightmare. He glanced behind Travis to where Roar sat between Kristen and Greyson. The lion winked.

"This place looks familiar," Travis said. "I feel as though I've been here before."

"Perhaps you have … in one of your dreams," Greyson said, snickering.

Floi pointed to the water and then to the forest that bordered the shoreline. "There's so much to be done to protect the White River. It's a source of recreation and provides water for a number of uses to all who live within the Indianapolis area. Pollution and runoff from fertilizers and pesticides create problems for fish, wildlife, and humans. But there's something you kids can do. And that's one of the reasons I've brought you here."

Squirrel saw a scattering of trash, so the grandmother's intention was clear. Plastic bottles, storage bags, and crushed soda cans lay among the exposed roots of trees and along the muddy shoreline.

He even saw a T-shirt like one that Travis wore and a single athletic shoe. The odor of rotting trash rose up from a plastic container, overpowering the scents of flowering plants in the wetland area. Squirrel figured humans had been careless, allowing things to fall into the water from the boats he'd seen when Travis and his cousins played near the river.

Floi handed each child a black bag and a pair of gloves. "You can clean up the area today. And each time you play here, look for ways to keep it clear of trash. It's something small you can do to help Pinkie keep Riverwood Hollow clean and healthy."

"Grandma, that's a great idea," added Kristen. "And we can research other ways to help. Maybe write letters and get involved in environmental organizations."

"We could create a neighborhood group called *Pinkie Opossum's Clean-Up Club*," Travis added.

"That's a wonderful idea," Floi said. "I was hoping you kids might find a way to do service for your community this summer."

Greyson held up Roar. "I'll be keeping watch over you, making sure you clean up all the trash." He made the lion's mouth roar in the next breath.

Travis held Squirrel up and made his mouth move. "I'm really good at gathering things and putting them in buried places—today, right in the trash." Squirrel's tail spiked with excitement. He had a special role in the kids' effort to clean up Riverwood Hollow.

Floi stepped out of the golf cart as Travis set Squirrel on the seat with Wings. "If you can imagine a world with talking puppets," she said, "you can dream a way to take care of the planet where you live."

Squirrel imagined the rest of the summer, scampering through Riverwood Hollow with his family. He would always be a real squirrel no matter which world he played in, and now he finally knew his dream was a real place. As Fire had once said, he could return there whenever he wanted.

Epilogue

Twenty Years Later

The most beautiful things in the world cannot be
seen or touched, they are felt with the heart.

—Antoine de Saint-Exupery, *The Little Prince*

The sky blushed with shades of pink and gold as the plane flew over the Indianapolis skyline. The early-morning flight from Chicago had been brief, and Travis was grateful to fly rather than make the four-hour drive.

While the plane made its final approach to the airport, he gazed out the window. Seeing the Soldiers and Sailors Monument, he thought about how some landmarks had remained unchanged over the years. The White River flowed through his old northside neighborhood near Broad Ripple. Then it made its way into the downtown area around the Indianapolis Zoo and Indiana State Museum. The capitol building and Indianapolis Motor Speedway were also visible from the window of the plane.

It would be a long day with his grandmother's funeral at Crown Hill Cemetery and the family gathering that would follow. Travis felt a strange sense of poignancy, remembering the days he had spent with his cousins years ago, trekking through Riverwood Hollow, playing with animal puppets and making up stories about a dream world. Pinkie Opossum's Clean-Up Club had become an ongoing community effort, thanks to his grandmother. He still had one of the original T-shirts. In all those years, he never imagined he'd become a professor of children's literature and theater at a major university.

He and his cousins, Greyson and Kristen, had kept in close contact over the years, and the families had shared Christmas holidays together. Greyson was coaching college football, and Kristen had become an environmental lawyer. His father was working at the same law firm, and his mother taught art at a local high school. Tobias, his younger brother, was attending Butler University.

When the plane began its descent, Travis looked at his wife, Marybeth, dozing in the aisle seat. He was glad she couldn't see the tears that had formed in his eyes.

*

After the funeral, Travis went to his grandmother's cottage, while Marybeth took the rest of the family to lunch. He wanted to spend time alone, honoring the memories of his grandmother and their magical times in Riverwood Hollow.

Lofty sycamore trees lined the sandy path along the White River where the old cottage stood, quaint as ever. The white siding had been recently painted and the roof replaced. The river shoreline was thick with orange lilies. Pansies lined the sidewalk, and a goddess statue ready with bow and arrows stood among Queen Anne ferns. An antique iron bench sat next to the entrance, and a flowered wreath hung on the front door. Travis wondered who had planted the flowers and kept the yard so clean and tidy.

Slipping the old-fashioned key into the front door lock, he noticed a dream catcher hanging from a hook beneath the tiny leaded window. "Of course," he whispered. "The dream world."

Once inside, he paused, inhaling the scent of lavender. Then he went straight to the kitchen. He opened the refrigerator, removed a bottle of root beer, and twisted off the cap. He found his favorite snack in the adjacent cabinet. "Yes, Oreos," he said. Ripping away the top of the package, he headed to his childhood bedroom.

When he opened the door, his eyes were drawn to the window seat opposite the iron bed where he had slept during his frequent visits. All the puppets, in near perfect repair, were lined up as though they were waiting for him to play with them again.

Travis picked up the smaller squirrel. He buried his face in the fur of his childhood friend, imagining the scent of the wetland forest where they had played. "We never found you a name, did we?" he said. "But I have a feeling you liked the name Squirrel."

Turning toward the bed, Travis plopped down on the quilted comforter and closed his eyes. He heard his own snore just before dropping into a dream.

*

A cool breeze ruffled his hair as his feet slipped on wet leaves. Mature oak trees formed a tunnel over the path leading away from his grandmother's side yard into a wildlife sanctuary. Exiting the portal of twined branches, he stepped onto a gravel road. It curved along the familiar forest on his right, where a full moon was setting. On his left, morning sunlight splashed gold over a field of clover and yellow wildflowers.

"I'm dreaming," Travis said, surveying the scene before him. "And it's just like I remember."

Lily pads covered the surface of the small pond at the end of the road where a blue heron waded in the shallows. With steady patience, the bird lifted one leg and then the other as she snuck up on fish swimming below the water's surface. Dragonflies buzzed the shorelines, some alighting on the ends of twigs, their wings glittering like precious jewels.

Travis heard a chittering call from the middle of the field next to the road. He moved toward the fire ring and the apple tree that was much larger than he remembered. Sitting down on a stump next to the tree, he sighed.

"I've been waiting for you."

"Who said that?" Travis asked, looking up.

In the next moment, a silver apple dropped to the ground. A squirrel sitting on a branch over his head flicked a bushy red tail and descended down the trunk of the tree. The puppet that had been in his arms when Travis fell asleep now sat at his feet.

"You remember me, don't you?" Squirrel said.

"Yes, but it's just a dream, isn't it?"

"Does this place seem real to you? How about this apple?" Squirrel said, picking up the apple.

Travis hesitated, scanning the scene beyond the pond. "Yes, but ..."

"This is a real place," Squirrel said. After taking a bite of the apple and dropping it, he continued. "One where I dreamed, where you and I dreamed together. And where all the puppets and your cousins played for many years."

Travis felt tears well up in his eyes. "I remember."

Squirrel stood up on his hind legs and pointed to the end of the gravel road. "Hey, remember that old mailbox?"

Travis followed Squirrel to the mailbox that stood next to the pond where the heron now held a fish in his beak. "We used to call it the magic mailbox," he said.

Squirrel climbed the shiny post and stretched himself across the top of the box. Spreading his front paws around the red flag that was placed in an upright position, he looked at Travis. "Maybe there's something inside that's meant for you."

Travis paced around the mailbox, assessing its possible contents "An old lady once told me that if the red flag is up, the box holds mail for the person who stands next to it."

"Ah yes. The lady who always had a pocket of four-leaf clovers in her skirt and a bag of fancy mixed nuts. Your grandmother."

Travis opened the door. Inside he saw an envelope and pulled it out. It was addressed to him, "To the boy named Travis c/o Riverwood Hollow." He inserted his index finger beneath the flap of the envelope and slid it through the seal. He lifted the yellowed paper out of the envelope, unfolded it, and read the words at the top of the page.

"'Adventures are for courageous souls.' It's a map, like the one I found in this box when I was a kid. I'll never forget that dream. They're the same words I read then."

"Hey, Travis! It's really you. And my little squirrel friend too!"

Travis turned. His grandmother stood tall and straight beneath a shower of golden light. Her face glowed with rosy health, and her eyes twinkled as though she was about to share important information with him, as she once did in a childhood dream. Travis felt the beat of his heart quicken.

"Grandma Floi? You startled me. It can't be true."

"Yes, dear. I thought I might find you here."

"You look different, like the younger photos I've seen of you."

"A dream has a way of doing that," his grandmother said while adjusting the silver combs in her upswept blonde hair.

"You're still wearing purple running shoes."

"Running is easier now, and I've always loved the color purple."

"But, Grandma, you're dead!"

"I once heard someone say, 'The afterlife is like living in another room of God's great house.' Even though I'm in that other room, I'm always available to you. Do you remember this world where as a child you played with Squirrel and his friends?"

"I do. I even taught Tobias about Riverwood Hollow."

His grandmother laughed. "It's in God's house too."

"Maybe that's why the Hollow has always been a magical place for us kids."

"And filled with miracles, I might add. Soon you will have your own son. You'll have the opportunity to pass along the message on the map. It takes courage to live in your world with all its challenges. But imagination helps a child open the magic mailbox and find his own personal map for navigating a life with love."

Travis stared at his grandmother, wondering if he would be a good father. "Grandma, I love you."

"You can always find me here," she said, touching his heart center. "If you remember to stay close to your dreams."

"I'll remember," Travis said.

The words were still on his lips as he awoke to the light spilling through the window from the setting sun. He felt a stirring of fur in his arms. When he glanced down, Squirrel winked.

Acknowledgments

Carol A. Paddock for boundless dedication, editing each draft with heart-centered generosity and eye for detail. Laurie Szpot for professional insights that pointed me in the right directions early in the editing process. Lorie Lee Andrews for illuminating the magic of Riverwood Hollow with stunning imagery. Helen Mozzi for steadfast encouragement during our writing sessions. Robert Moss, teacher, guide, and friend, for the practices of his original Active Dreamwork. Dwayne Dixon for his photographic assistance. Jennifer Foley for enduring friendship through the process. My family, Kent Eastwood, Colton Eastwood, Rowan Eastwood, Tobin Eastwood, and Brand Russell-Eastwood, for loving support and counsel that helped me bring this fanciful tale to print.

Made in the USA
Middletown, DE
04 December 2021

54192215R00132